Wilderness Road

Wilderness Road

Lauran Paine

Thorndike Press • Chivers Press
Thorndike, Maine USA   Bath, England

This Large Print edition is published by Thorndike Press, USA and by Chivers Press, England.

Published in 2000 in the U.S. by arrangement with Golden West Literary Agency.

Published in 2000 in the U.K. by arrangement with Golden West Literary Agency.

U.S. Hardcover 0-7862-2578-5 (Basic Collection Edition)
U.K. Hardcover 0-7540-4190-5 (Chivers Large Print)
U.K. Softcover 0-7540-4191-3 (Camden Large Print)

The text of this Large Print edition is unabridged.
Other aspects of the book may vary from the original edition.

Set in 16 pt. Plantin by Rick Gundberg.

Printed in the United States on permanent paper.

British Library Cataloguing in Publication Data available

Library of Congress Cataloging-in-Publication Data

Paine, Lauran.
    Wilderness road / Lauran Paine.
        p.   cm.
    ISBN 0-7862-2578-5 (lg. print : hc : alk. paper)
    1. Nevada — Fiction. 2. Large type books. I. Title.
PS3566.A34 W55 2000
813'.54—dc21   00-029914

Wilderness Road

CHAPTER ONE

There Is Only Tomorrow

Reilly pushed the jug over in the dust. It left squiggly tracks. "Here, Mort. You need one."

The younger man hefted the jug in a sweeping, experienced lift and drank. Reilly's squinted eyes counted the swallows. Six of them. "There's alcohol in that," he said dryly, then shrugged and glanced away. It didn't matter; Mort needed that drink. Those drinks. If a man had a right to get sick-drunk it was Morton Ramsey. It wasn't every day a man killed his brother.

Reilly retrieved the jug and shoved the cork in it. Flies had a monotonous habit of committing suicide in whisky crocks in the summer-time. Mort spoke finally, without actually looking into Reilly's seamed face.

"Aren't you going to have one?"

"Had one before. One's enough for me."

"Oh; you figure I need more?"

Reilly squirmed his bottom on the hard ground. They were alone down by the barn. The air was dry enough to light a match with. The sun hung murderously in the washed-out sky and the range shimmered under a heat lashing that left everything wilted and dying.

"Cut it out," Reilly said in his quiet, patient way, understanding how the younger man felt and trying gently to soothe him out of it.

"Pat, will you go over and turn my horses out?"

"Sure. Ride over this evening. How long'll you be away, Mort?"

"I don't know," Mort said vaguely. "Hell — I don't know." He glanced at the dust on his boots; it was like the ground — grey and lifeless and suffering-looking. "Maybe six, eight months, Pat. If I'm not back in a year, keep 'em."

"Mort" — Reilly spoke softly without changing his glance from a slit-eyed contemplation of the heat-ridden land; didn't look at the younger man at all — "don't run away, boy. It can't be done. Try it an' the damned memories'll haunt you to hell and back."

"Who's running?"

"Well — what're you leaving for?"

No answer. Somewhere around in back of Pat Reilly's bleached-out old barn a horse blew his nose lustily.

Reilly got up stiffly, massaged one leg with a grimace. "Reckon I'd better go up to the house. Carrie'll be ringing that damned bell pretty quick. I hate that thing; seems like my life's run by that old bell."

"Wait a second, Pat." Mort didn't look up or say anything else. Pat hadn't moved. Now he wouldn't. He was an infinitely patient man anyway. Summer evenings were long. He could do his chores an hour later without any fuss or inconvenience.

Time dragged. The smell of the hot land was like sulphur ashes to them. The barn had an aroma of combined smells that were good, especially in the shade where they sat with the two-toned crockery jug between them.

"Pat — you want to hear how it happened?"

"Not 'specially. Expect I'll hear soon enough in town."

"Yeah," Mort said quickly, "that's just it. I don't give a hoot how most folks hear it, but I want you to get it straight."

"All right," Pat Reilly said; "shoot."

"I was in Will Harper's saloon when the sheriff came in and rounded up a posse. No one knew who we were after until we'd been sworn in and led out."

Pat Reilly interrupted long enough to

swear blisteringly about the sheriff. He wound it up with a long, resigned sort of a sigh. Mort went on:

"Dell Forrest and I hit the kid's trail at Papage Springs. The others went back after a while. Dell and I kept going. The kid was holed up at Dead Water. His horse had played out. We saw the damned horse first. Dell shot it. It was dying. Darned kid never did know how to ride a horse; never did. Anyway, Dell's shot brought the kid up shooting. His second shot knocked Dell flat. I ran over to Dell and the kid hollered at me. Called me everything he could lay his tongue to and tried to get me. I got Dell back in among the boulders, but he'd been hard hit. Blood was running out of his mouth like a stream. He looked up and said, 'Mort, that's your brother. By God, Mort, that's Jay. Dammit — a man shouldn't kill his own brother!' Dell died right after that. I made a cigarette."

"Jay still in the rocks?"

"Yeah. Cussing like he'd gone crazy and shooting into the boulders trying to find me. Pat — it's an awful feeling. Your brother trying to kill you, a good friend dead beside you, and there you are, holed up like a drunk In'ian, scairt to sit and scairt to run and all sort of mixed up inside."

10

"You talk to him?"

"Talk to him?" Mort's sunken eyes lifted and stayed on Pat Reilly's profile. "I didn't kill him in cold blood, Pat."

"I didn't mean that, Mort. Take another drink, boy."

"In a minute. Sure; I called over to him. Reminded him of a lot of stuff just he and I knew about. Like the times we made cornhusk cigarettes and stole Old Man Levin's rupture belt and hid it. It didn't do any good. He had me pinned down and wouldn't let up. I tried every way I could think of. None of it worked, Pat. All he'd say was that his own brother was in the posse that came out to run him down. I tried to reason with him. Nothing worked. Not a damned thing. I stayed down and sweated; ached all over. It seemed like dark'd never come. When it did I never had a chance to slip away. He came over those rocks like a catamount. Pat — I had to. God Almighty — I had to. Right through the brisket at a hundred feet. Jay never knew what hit him."

"You made sure?"

Mort almost groaned. "Hell, Pat," he said protestingly, "I never went over; didn't have to. Just turned and walked away. I could see one leg dangling over a big rock. That was enough."

The tiniest of all breezes ruffled the powder-fine dust around them with a languid, sluggish movement, but it wasn't refreshing at all. Just made their clothes feel all the stiffer from salt-sweat.

Reilly pushed the jug over. Mort hefted it and drank again, spat against the ground and breathed through his mouth to escape the medicine taste of the whisky. Silence descended between them like a thick wall. Settled into the barn even, and seemed to clog up Pat Reilly's nostrils. He took up the jug and drank out of it, then hit the cork hard with the palm of his hand.

"Damnation!" he said savagely.

"Pat, you care if I bed down in your barn tonight? I'm about sucked dry and burnt out."

"No, not in the barn. In the house."

Mort Ramsey shook his head. "No. Hell — I've got a bed at home. I just want to sleep out here tonight."

Pat didn't agree or disagree. He switched the subject. "How about Tassie?"

No answer again. Pat ran a hand over the turkey-red, criss-crossed hide that was the back of his weathered neck. Massaged the back of his head and kneaded the tightly strung tendons back there.

"You want me to tell her? Is that it, Mort?"

12

"It'd be better that way, wouldn't it, Pat?"

"I don't think so," Reilly said evenly, then he lapsed into a long silence and seemed to be considering his own answer for a while. Then he shrugged slightly. "All right. Maybe. In the morning."

Mort had wanted him to ride to Clearwater and see the girl that night, before she heard it from others. Jay had hung around the girl a lot. She was pretty, too. Mort had liked her once, before Jay came into the country and sort of took over; after that Mort had stayed away. Tassie Clement . . .

"That's why you told me how it happened, isn't it, Mort? So's I'd have it straight for her?"

"Not exactly. So's you and Carrie'd know how it happened, too, Pat. You've been like folks to me since I settled hereabouts."

Pat grunted, squirmed gingerly on the hard ground and made a face. One of his feet had gone to sleep; now it ache-tickled when he moved. "I'll beat that damned bell by one second. Here — you keep the jug down here."

"Don't tell Carrie I'm here, Pat. She'll come down."

"Yeah." Pat grunted to his feet, hobbled

13

gingerly for a minute in a stamping little circle, straightened finally and headed for the house, without another word.

Mort Ramsey took care of his gaunt horse, flung his bedroll down in the hay and went out back for a last smoke before he rolled in. The sun was dipping fast, like a vertical bowl of watered blood. Dropping over the edge of the world and leaving the panting earth of Nevada behind it. He stood there with his thoughts, unconscious of any way to turn them off. Jay Ramsey, his brother, a stage robber. Every thought prompted another one. That's where the money came from that Jay always had to burn. The silver on his saddle and the inlay on his gun. The easy arrogance of him.

Jay was dead. His only living kin dead, and he'd killed him. And the yesterdays since he'd come to the Clearwater country, liked it and stayed, were dead too, for the stain of Cain would haunt him as long as he stayed. The years he'd played starve-out with cattle prices. The shed-sweat he'd put into every log of his house, barn and corrals. The long hours he'd put into earning cash for his cattle herd. It was all behind him now. In its stead was an acute sense of aloneness.

He thought back to the day Jay had ridden

in with his tied-down gun and big, wide smile. He remembered the challenging brown eyes and the lock of curly auburn hair dangling below a thumbed-back black hat. Mort had sensed something hard and illogical in that scarcely known younger brother then. Had often wondered about it, too; wondered what had made the kid like he was, and he'd never know now. The lost years of Jay Ramsey's existence were something they never discussed.

He smoked, thinking back over a jumble of unpleasantness that was his own early life as an orphan in a raw land, and knew Jay's days had been no better; maybe even worse. Something had made Jay the way he was, and it had cost him his life. If dead Dell Forrest could have killed him though, it would have been so much better; but no, it had to be Mort who did it. Killed his own brother over a lousy stage messenger's pouch of new money. Kinship meant more than anything else in those early days in Nevada. The men had little use for law and order anyway, so it was clannishness that held them together, protected them and was foremost in their eyes. Those who enforced the law were seldom popular either, for the land was harsh and life was very real to the few who inhabited it. Terrible winters and waterless summers. Sandstorms and freeze-out and dust devils; not the usual spring, summer, fall and winter.

The people were fierce in their stubborn hatreds too. They detested outfits like the Big Sink Stage Company out of hand. It wasn't envy, it was hatred. The kind that comes to any people who labour to exhaustion for a grubbed-out living while others make money without labouring.

There were outlaws by the score, Eagles like Jay Ramsey. Men with courage and quick guns. There were scavengers too; human buzzards who bushwhacked and knifed in the night. All kinds of men. Eagles, buzzards, cowmen, gamblers, lawmen and what not, the code of survival was the same. Shoot fast and straight, ride light and rest your horse often, and hate any man who would turn on his own, for kinship meant everything in a country where everything but a brother or cousin was hostile. Hate any man who would turn on his own . . .

Mort stomped out the cigarette and stood against the doorless opening at the back of Pat Reilly's barn. One gunshot had wiped out everything he had sweated for. One single gunshot. He heard a horse loping in the dusk and turned to gaze north-westward. It was Reilly heading toward

16

Mort's stump-patch ranch to turn the horses out.

The sun was gone. A twilight lingered and lingered, started rusty-red and ran the spectrum to a deep, lasting purple. The heat remained and the heaven was tinted with a lightish hue. Mort looked at it. Where, up there, would a man like Jay go? A shot-down stage robber, part of some rotten gang, who was hardly twenty-one years old and as snarling hard as iron in his heart and soul. Always handsome. Mort remembered the dark good looks and thought Jay had never honestly had a chance. Never. And if he *had* had one, being really good-looking like he was was something not very many men could overcome. Certainly not a kid like Jay. To kill your own brother . . .

Horses. Reilly returning. No — Mort moved swiftly, deeper into the darkness outside the barn. Reilly went alone. This new sound had the hollow thunder to it of several horses punishing the hard ground. Instinct made him melt into the shadows. Instinct and a fragment he recalled of an old conversation with a hermit in a cabin high in the pine forest of the Great Divide country. "When in doubt, boy, hide out." Sound advice. He heard the horses lope by and fetch up over by the house. Softly the rattle of rein chains and spur rowels drifted to him across the night air, then voices, not loud, but loud enough.

"Miz Reilly? Yes'm. . . . No, haven't seen hide nor hair of Pat. Well — we dassen't stay that long, thanks, ma'm. Was just wonderin' ef you folks seen Morton Ramsey. We come from his place . . . he ain't there."

Mort heard Carrie Reilly's voice. It was a pitch higher than usual. Tight sounding. "What do you want him for?"

For a moment she got no answer, then a booming voice farther back among the silhouettes who were horsemen spoke out. "We want a man'd kill his own brother. Man'd do that. . . ."

"Yes. You want lynch law, don't you? Well — he's not here, but I wish Pat was."

One of the riders laughed suddenly, bit it off quickly, so abruptly it made Mort's flesh crawl. He watched them depart, riding in a long lope, bunched up a little, greyer in the gloom than the night was. Then he saddled one of Pat's horses and rode shuffingly towards his own place, a sickening premonition full grown within him. Lynchers, nightriders, whatever they were and whoever they were, Mort Ramsey's life was in the balance and Pat Reilly was implicated,

18

too, for no other reason than because he was a friend of a man who'd killed his own brother. A good neighbour and a staunch friend.

Cannily, Mort drew up on the far side of the long, undulating landswell that kept a lot of the winter drifts out of the little meadow along Willow Creek, where his ranch was. He tied the Reilly horse under a shaggy juniper tree and shucked his spurs. There wasn't a sound down there by his loghouse or the barn either. Not a single sound. Hunching away from the skyline, he went in a great circle and came up to the rear of his barn from the south. The smell of horses was strong there, but not an animal was in the corral. Pat had already turned them out. Then he was either riding homeward, maybe even stepping down in his own barn right then, or he hadn't left the Ramsey place. Maybe they had passed unheard in the night. Mort didn't think they had, but he hoped so.

What kept him outside the barn, though, was the deathly stillness of the place. Like the world was holding its breath. No crickets, no night birds; not a sound. It made the flesh crawl along the back of his neck. Palms damp and oily, Mort lowered himself to the dusty, pungent earth and skylined the cabin around a corner of the barn. There was no movement there at all, but neither were there any of the noises he had come to expect every night. Sounds like the frog that hung around the spring-box and croaked every night without exception — unless. . . .

Unless the night-riders were novices — which he knew they weren't. So that meant they'd left a bushwhacker at the ranch in case the others missed Mort. The smell of a stranger on the place would account for the stillness. They got used to the smell of one man all the time. A stranger would make them stealthy with apprehension. Mort lay flat, thinking. Somewhere around the Ramsey ranch — somewhere in the soft stillness and unearthly gloom — was a man with a gun, waiting.

He speculated, then swore under his breath. If the night wasn't dark enough, there were too many shadows. Angles and corners and shadowy depths where the sentinel could hide, and Mort couldn't wait. Not with the strong possibility that the lynchers would ride back to see if he'd been home, or to pick their henchman up on the way back to Clearwater.

The barn was stifling hot inside. He moved very slowly, eyes squared against the hush and blackness of the log building, squinting into the murkiness for sign that the man with the gun might be inside. He wasn't, though. Mort knew he wouldn't be — knew why, too — when he'd made his careful way up to the middle of the building, up where the saddle-pole was, and straightened up very slowly.

The huge baulk he'd raised into place as the cross-beam above the doorless opening made an opalescent foreground for the lighter darkness beyond the doorway. From it, turning ever so gently around and a half, then swinging back just as methodically, was a man suspended from the baulk by a lariat. He was dead. Mort didn't need a closer look. It was in the lazy, quiet way he turned. In the macabre angle of his head. A grotesque cant that has no counterpart among the living.

He forgot the gun in his hand. The danger that lay like a blind rattler somewhere beyond the barn in the still night, and the sickening ache that was in his entrails over Jay. He stood motionless, staring. Recognition wasn't possible from where he stood, but he didn't have to go any closer. Pat Reilly. Rugged, whimsical, tolerant, aging Pat Reilly.

An overwhelming near-blindness seized

him. An illness he had never experienced before. It was as though the purple night was a black fist pressing down on him, forcing him to kneel on the stone-hard adobe underfoot. And when the ague passed, fury came up in its stead. Pounding up into his head; beating at his temples until he could taste the acid bitterness of every heartbeat. Pat Reilly. . . . First Jay, then Pat. If he'd asked who the posse was after that morning, Jay wouldn't have been killed by his brother. If he hadn't asked Pat to turn out his horses because he didn't want to go back to the ranch he had shared with his brother, Carrie wouldn't be a widow.

Somewhere out in the night was a man who would know who did that to Pat. Might even be the one who had stood Pat on his saddle, then quirted the horse out from under him. Mort Ramsey didn't think beyond that one man. Didn't realise he was willing, eager even, to compound a murder. Didn't care. . . .

It took a long time to work a half-mile circle around the house and come in from behind it. It took almost as long to travel through the willows without making any noise and get close enough to the back of his cabin to have solid protection. Then he knew his guess had been right. Only one animal on earth made that smell; a human animal. It was the tangy odour of tobacco smoke that hung low in the hot night and clung to the house area. Mort felt no triumph. He lay flat and tried to guess where the man was.

Not in the house, he could tell that by the looks of things. The big brass padlock hung untouched on the hasp. Maybe over by the dilapidated little chicken-house he'd built hopefully — and the skunks and racoons had raided so consistently that he had given up the wish for eggs for breakfast. Or beyond that, out in the dried grass somewhere, belly-down and waiting. No; he wasn't that far away. No gunman would bother to hide that well — then smoke.

He turned and crawled back into the willows, went south toward the barn a little ways, almost to the end of the rank growth, then flattened again. Then came the feeling of savage exultation. The man wasn't over by the chicken-house after all. He was up ahead somewhere, among the willows. It wasn't so much the fragrance of the tobacco that made Mort certain, now. It was a new smell any blind rider could identify on any hot night. Horse sweat.

A picture of the ambusher grew steadily behind his eyes. The man was lazy; he was also probably callous. Too stupid or indifferent to be really dangerous — the tobacco smoke told Mort that much as he lay there, hardly daring to breathe. His eyes stung from forehead sweat. He blinked the stuff away and studied the area around the willows.

Faintly, the grisly shapelessness of dead Pat Reilly dangled in the doorway of the barn. The bushwhacker had chosen a spot where he could command a view of the dead man and the approaches to him, from the front.

Mort's lips curled downwards. No one but a green-grass pilgrim would have ridden up in plain sight and cut Pat down. He inched up a little. The man ahead was no killer; maybe he was a Clearwater drunk or a range-tramp; mean and sneaky and dangerous from behind; but he surely wasn't a gunman by trade. If he had been, he'd have been blasted away from his buckles long ago. He inched forward. The loudest sound right then was the drumroll of his own heartbeats inside him.

The sentinel was sitting cross-legged, hat far back; thick, coarse profile toward the open country beyond the ranchyard. Mort saw him only because he was looking for him. In the background behind the man a horse stood drowsing, rawhide reins and romal looped carelessly over a bent willow the size of a man's wrist. Both were motionless with languor. The snout of Mort's gun came up very slowly. His aim would have to be perfect the first time, because the man would hear him cock the single-action .45 seconds before he tugged off the shot. A final, fleeting glance at the pale blob that was the man's face, filigreed in the leafy shadows. It wasn't an old face, but it looked old in the gloom, with hollows filled up to overflowing with shadow, and hooded eyes mirroring boredom that was bottomless.

"Don't wiggle a finger, hombre. Steady!"

The man's reaction was sudden. He went rigid, but he obeyed. Didn't even turn his head. The carbine across his knees quivered once when a brace of convulsive fingers brushed it, and that was all.

"Reach up with both hands," Mort said quietly, "and push that hat off, then lock your fingers on top of your head and stand up."

The stranger complied and had to smother a grunt, for he'd been sitting like that a long time. Mort got up, too, edged in behind him, swooped with one hand and tossed the man's belt-gun into the willows and nudged him out into the yard beyond the willows.

"That's good; hold it. Not too far out. Who did that?"

"Did what?"

A vicious sideways slam of Mort's gun-barrel over the man's kidneys knocked him to his knees. He let off one deep, anguished cry.

"Who did that?"

"I don't — hell! — are you Ramsey?"

Mort had just one thing in mind. He moved swiftly. The stranger saw his face in the watery light and cried out in terror. The noise stopped Mort in mid-stride.

"I didn't do it. I — didn't see 'em do it, hones' to —"

"You're a liar! You think I'm going to horse around with you?"

"No — lissen, Ramsey — hones' t'God. I was with the horses —" It trailed off. The man could see what lay ahead of him, any way he turned. He made a clumsy, wild lunge for Mort's legs, grasped one and yanked with all the one-armed strength of desperation. Mort went to his knees, caught a large fist high on his forehead and swung the gun with all his might, as though the thing were a club. His face was indescribably ugly with its stain of blood-lust. The ambusher went over sideways in the dust. Blood, like black oil in the darkness, ran thickly through his hair. Mort stared at him, turned abruptly on his heel and went back to the horse in the willows, untied the animal and brought him up to the dying man, took down the lariat from the saddle-swells and flicked out a little calf-loop.

It didn't take fifteen minutes to do the grisly job, but Mort was wringing wet from the effort, for neither man was light and both were limp to handle. Pat Reilly was tied athwart the bushwhacker's saddle and the stranger was dangling from the baulk in his place. The hanging man was still twitching when Mort hauled him up. If he wasn't dead it didn't matter; he'd die without knowing how.

All the way back to the Reilly place Mort's mind was suffused with a sense of primitive satisfaction. Frontier justice well and ironically meted out. Vengeance deserved and taken. And normalcy didn't return to him until Carrie Reilly's first wild cry echoed through the night. Then it came with all the stored-up horror of what he'd done, right from the moment he'd squeezed off the fatal shot at his renegade brother.

He couldn't stand the Reilly place, either, any more than he could stand the thought of his own place with that thing dangling in the entrance to the barn. Walking woodenly

27

and without looking back, he went to the barn, changed his saddle to his own horse, swung up with the muffled, abandoned shrieks of that hair-raising grief coming through the close, hot night to him, and reined out over the dying, sunblasted range, neither knowing nor caring which way his horse went.

The seconds multiplied into massive hours that dragged themselves by on crippled, leaden feet. The night was a haunted cavern of no ending; close, sweaty, so silent it hurt his ears, and inhabited by twin phantoms who kept pace on either side of him and never once looked around, although he knew they had deep reproach in their eyes.

He was still riding like that at sun-up. Aimlessly, far south and east of Clearwater. Drifting along on the oily tide of a life made hateful to him by those two profiles that wouldn't turn and look him in the face. The other face — the man he'd hung in Pat's place — wasn't even remembered. It would never be a face or a body, only a symbol of savagery he had given way to. There wouldn't ever be remorse over that one, anyway; frontier justice sustained — demanded — what he had done there. Perhaps not as he had done it, but a lot of hard-eyed men would have a flicker of sardonic amusement over that, too.

Then, one tangible effect reached through Mort's grey world. The sunshine. It came out of the east and poured molten misery down over the parched lips of the world and on to the bosom below. Spread fiery desolation fanning outward from the source until everything was panting that could pant, and what could not, writhed and drooped away. The rider noticed his horse grow listless. Grow heavy in the bit. Shuffle-footed and ungainly in his movement. Almost without awareness, Mort headed him towards the nearest shade, which happened to be a sagebrush hill with some scraggly fir trees on its crest.

But the desert country is different from the watershed lands. Shade on the desert means less eye-ache but no coolness. The horse glistened with water even under the old trees. Mort lay down looking dully out over the country he had ridden over. Watched it shimmer and waver and bleach out. Hating it for everything it had made him labour so hard to get, then ruthlessly snatched away from him in the space of one long summer day.

He smoked and thought of the stranger he'd hit with his gun and hung. Try as he might he could not recollect the man's face at all. The ambusher was a symbol. He had killed it — the symbol, not the man. And there was Pat Reilly, who had become almost like the father neither of the Ramsey boys had ever known. Tough, gruff, wise old Pat. All wool and a yard wide. He'd done Mort Ramsey a little favour like he'd done a thousand times before, and it had cost him his life. Mort inhaled deeply. He could imagine old Pat's back stiffening. He'd seen Reilly get that way before. And, before Pat had a chance, some liquored-up cowboy had snaked out a little calf-loop, draped it over Pat's head. . . . Carrie: what must she be thinking of Mort Ramsey, the man who sent her husband to his death.

"Jay," he said out loud. "Jay — yes. But not Pat Reilly."

He made another cigarette, lit it off the stub of the old one, and leaned back in the sodden griminess of his shirt and smoked all over again. Eyes tightened into long, narrow slits against the murderous sungouge; staring, but not seeing exactly, over the breathless world of Paiute Valley; knowing that Clearwater would be north and a little west of him, among a clutch of wonderful shade trees, but unable to see it from where he was.

And the rider materialised out of the oppressive atmosphere as though he was riding a foot off the ground. Mort watched him moving steadily towards his knoll, and continued to smoke. One man meant two guns. A carbine and a belt-gun. They would be even. Mort shrugged away the thought. It didn't look right for that. When those who wanted him would come again, they would ride in a posse — and that was ironic, too; for Mort, the deputized lawman of yesterday, was the wanted killer of today. Not for Jay, but for the man he'd hung to the baulk of his barn. In the eyes of the law that man never had a chance. The fact that he'd tried wouldn't count, for there was only Mort Ramsey's word for that. Morton Ramsey, wanted murderer.

He dropped the cigarette and spat on it. Murderer. The idea hadn't occurred to him before. Lawman one day, outlaw the next day. He looked up squint-eyed and watched the rider without thinking about him at all. Yesterday a comfortable, industrious, small cowman with only one worry that was a wild, damfool kid. Yesterday he had something. Now he had his horse, two guns, and an impersonal deadliness.

The rider kept on coming. Mort knew he had seen the horse on the little hilltop and possibly the man squatting beneath and in front of the animal. Either the rider didn't know who Mort Ramsey was, or hadn't recognised him, because he held towards the knoll as steadily as his horse would travel, riding in Mort's own tracks. It wasn't until the big, raw-boned Appaloosa horse with his leopard-marked rump and ugly head came close enough that Mort knew the rider with a deep jolt, and shoved upright in astonishment. Stood like a statue sculptured out of the grey dust and strong sweat that covered him, and stared.

The Appaloosa horse came on. Mort could hear him grunt his way up the hill. Heard the wiry snap-back of the tenacious sage. Heard pebbles roll away over ground drawn dry and drumhead tight. Then he heard the voice, and it was like melting snow — water running over shiny rocks in an upland creek somewhere.

"Mort — Mort!"

He said nothing, noticing the glassiness of her stare and the warning with its too-bright red splotches over the cheekbones.

"They're all hunting for you, Mort."

"Yeah," he said flatly. "How'd you find me?"

She reined up and swung down as though the effort of dismounting took her last ounce of energy. "I didn't find you, I followed you. Been following for hours. Ever since you left Reilly's. I knew you'd get in touch with them some time, so I rode out from town."

"Why?"

The girl's colour mellowed in the shade, but her eyes were ringed with indelible purple etchings. "I wanted to hear it from you. That you really shot your own brother."

Mort took a fierce hold on the anger that was pushing up into his throat. "Didn't you like what the others told you? Jay's dead. By now they've hauled his body into Clearwater. You've probably seen it yourself. Been told, maybe, what he looks like now. All you had to know was that he's dead. That's all. What's the difference to you how it happened? Whether one posseman or another did it? He's dead. That's all you have to know, Tassie. Jay — Ramsey — is — dead!"

"Mort" — she left it hanging there a second — "why did you shoot him?"

He swore like a log-jam giving way before the backed-up pressure of the years, letting words roll out staccato swift, blistering and helplessly. "I killed him, Tassie, because I had no other choice. I shot him when he was

33

running at me — shooting. One of us had to die. It was Jay. Does that answer you?"

She was easily seven years younger than he was, but the stamp of character, of courage and anguish was as plain in one as the other. He had never known her awfully well. Had considered her Jay's girl and had looked no further, although inside he'd never gotten over the times they had danced together either. Now he felt a little of the same turmoil he'd known when he'd laid Pat Reilly out on his bed and heard that first blood-curdling scream from Carrie. Only Tassie hadn't been married to Jay. She didn't have a lifetime of recollections like the older woman had. Still, he felt about the same.

"Your own brother — Mort." The futility of anything she'd say overwhelmed her. The next sentence died with his name.

A peculiar calm came over him abruptly. A sort of resignation and weariness beyond fathoming. It made his eyes gentle to match his voice. "Tassie, listen to me. Jay killed Dell Forrest. I drug Dell back into the rocks. Tassie, I tried to talk Jay out of it. He was kill-crazy; I can't explain it. Anyway, he came out of those boulders like a drunk In'ian, hollering and shooting. I shot back. I had to. That's all there was to it."

"And the man hanging in your barn, Mort?"

He looked straight at her without blinking. "I don't know what to say about him. Did you ever see a man who's been like your own flesh and blood hanging to a barn rafter, Tassie. Strung up for absolutely nothing at all except that he happened to be doing a neighbour a favour when the wolves came on to him? Ever see a man you thought the world and all of strangled to death by a damned drunk night-rider's lariat?"

She didn't answer any of his questions. "In town they say he was beaten half to death before you hung him. Mort — you must have been insane when you did that. Oh, Mort!"

He tossed his head with a curt, angry gesture. "There isn't anything I can say about that. I don't even remember what he looked like. He deserved exactly what he got, Tassie; besides, I didn't beat him half to death, as they say; only hit him once that I remember." He saw her high flush and knew it was the danger sign from too much sun. "First Jay, then Pat, Tassie. What was I supposed to do?"

"I don't know, Mort, but I know what you have to do now."

"Yeah; run like a dog, don't I?"

"Yes. Sheriff Walsh has a posse up. They're criss-crossing the range for you. I — don't think you'll be able to get away from him."

He shrugged. "Funny thing, Tassie; I don't care."

She slumped a little and moved in closer to the shade. "How could it happen like it did?" He made no sound. She watched his eyes rake out over the heat-scourged land indifferently almost, then come back to a steady, impassive scrutiny of her face.

"Mort — I want to tell you something. Jay and I had a serious quarrel last month. He didn't come back to the house. It was all over. We both knew it."

"Well," he said irritably, "that's water under the bridge. Why tell me, anyhow?"

"Because of the reason, Mort. He was riding with the Cameron boys."

"Trash," Mort said scornfully. "Just saloon trash."

"They're more than you think. That's why we quarrelled, Mort. They're stage robbers. Stage and bank robbers. Jay told me."

"He should have kept his damned mouth shut," Mort said harshly.

"Do you condone what they were doing — the Camerons and Jay?"

"Of course not; don't be silly. But — well

36

— Jay was different. Besides, I minded my own business."

"Maybe," she said, stung finally, "if you'd looked after Jay a little more, this wouldn't have happened."

That brought the haunted blue eyes back to her face again. He stared in silence for a while. The vein at the side of his neck was throbbing heavily. "Are you blaming me because Jay was an outlaw, Tassie, as well as blaming me for killing him?"

"No. I — just started out to tell you that I told Jay he and I were finished unless he stopped running with the Camerons."

"And he wouldn't quit, would he? Hell, Tassie, I could've told you Jay never obeyed an order in his life. It wasn't in him. He was wild. Always was, I reckon; always would've been." He looked past her, into a world of his own; down the twisted, obscure land of hectic memory.

"It used to make me sick, sometimes, watching that kid, Tassie. Like the time he was practising with his six-gun. Shot the forelegs off a doe and rode after her on his horse, making her run like the devil on those stumps. He never did finish her; I did." The blue eyes dropped to her face again. "He wouldn't have knuckled under for — for — you or anyone else, Tassie."

"For — God Almighty — you were going to say, weren't you?"

"Yeah."

"He'll have the chance. So will Lem Cameron. He was the man you hung last night."

"That so? He's the youngest of the Camerons, isn't he?"

"Yes. Grat and Davis are riding after you on their own. They wouldn't join up with Sheriff Walsh."

"No," Mort said dryly, "I don't reckon they would. They'd rather catch me and have their own necktie party."

"That's what I meant when I said I didn't think you'd get away. L. C. Walsh and a Clearwater posse hunting high and low for you. The Camerons tracking you in their own way, and —"

"And you — a girl — finding me. It looks too simple, doesn't it? Well, Tassie, you go on back to your lavender sachets and orderly life, and I'll keep moving —"

"South, Mort? You could go down into California and cross over into Mexico."

He made a mirthless, wry smile at her. "Tassie — you're a nice girl, and pretty; I always said you were. But Lord — you're dumb!"

"Why?"

"Mexico wouldn't save me. Sure it'd make the law haul up on the border, but even that isn't too sure. But the Camerons'll keep coming as long as they know I'm alive. Mexico or China, those boys'll follow me until hell freezes over, then chase me two days on the ice."

"Where *can* you go, then, Mort? You've got to keep moving, and you've got to go a long way from Clearwater. If —"

"No, ma'am. The Camerons want me and I want them. They hung Pat Reilly without a ghost of a chance. Without any reason at all except that Pat was my friend. And they didn't lead Jay astray, Tassie, but they sure as the devil got him into his last pickle. I don't want any revenge for Jay — but they do. They want my blood for their brother, too. No matter where I run, they'll hunt me down. I'll save the horses for both of us. I won't run. I might even get a mite of supper while they're getting dinner, too. It isn't as one-sided as it looks, Tassie. I owe them for Lem Cameron and they owe me for Pat Reilly. I didn't know it until you came along, but I know it now. I'm not going to run, Tassie. Thanks for clearing the thing up for me."

He went to his horse and swung up. She watched him, licked her dry lips and didn't move. The face he looked at her through was expressionless, like the eyes were, too. She began to shake her head very slightly, not so much in the dumb apathy that held her, but in a way that indicated vast bewilderment and fear. As though she was groping for something she couldn't understand or reach either.

"That's crazy, Morton Ramsey. It just isn't rational at all. One man against the Camerons and the law. It isn't even the kind of a thing a — a — fool would do. Unless you just don't care whether they kill you or not."

"That," he said flatly, with that odd, mirthless grin again, "might be about it, Tassie. A man grubs uphill all his life, then gets it all shot out from under him in one day. The incentive's gone, maybe; something sure is. Go on back, girl. Tell L.C. — "

"Tell him yourself," she said, moving swiftly towards her horse, toeing into the stirrup and riding off before she'd fully gotten the saddle.

He watched her go. The smile withered gradually and was gone. Only the long look without expression followed her. The look of a man facing extinction, knowing it, and determined to use every instinct he had to live long enough to settle a score.

He thought of Jay and sneered. Damned tinhorn with his silvered gun and fancy rigging. A brother could hope as long as such a man lived, like a mother might do, but when the wayward one died, so did all the hope. Then the bubble was burst and there was no point in clinging to the illusion.

"He wasn't any good, and maybe he never was. He never would've been; I know that. He'd of gotten it just like he did some day, anyway — only what kind of a Fate is there that makes a man kill his own brother?" He stared after the big-headed, spotted-rumped horse. "And her — like a husky little cornflower. She's either blind or dumb as hell. Jay was a four-flusher but she never saw through him; not until they broke up. She's a sort of a kid in the head, maybe."

He moved the horse and rode down the far side of the hill.

CHAPTER TWO

Draw and Be Damned!

The awareness of danger lay just under the surface with Mort. It always had, apparently. Life in the primitive land had done that; erased the barriers to violence that were the civilised man's inhibitions. He rode overland, conscious of how easily a man slips off the mantle of organised society and reverts to the instincts of a wolf.

And the world was an altogether different place to a hunted man. Once, he had ridden that range thinking in terms of livestock. Shade from heat, brush patches where critters could hide from the everlasting flies. Water-holes and grass. Now it was different. Two days of existence as a wanted man had made him look ahead for possible enemies. Study the hardpan for fresh tracks of manhunters, shy away from timbered canyons and keep to the high places, where that panorama of Paiute Valley lay naked all around.

When he slept it was hidden away like a bitch-bear at cubbing time. When he ate it was with a sense of time wasted. He moved and never stopped; circling, back-tracking, hiding and riding, always. A hunted man, Mort Ramsey adapted himself quickly to the instinctive rules that govern them.

And all the time his mind was working. Searching out ways of exacting payment in full for dead Pat Reilly. That was all he lived for. Beyond that he was vague in his mind. Indifferent, because he didn't think past his vengeance. Also, there was a core of belief that he wouldn't live beyond his revenge, so he ignored what came afterwards and concentrated on a way to find, and fight, the Camerons. Everything else was excluded from his mind with the single exception of Sheriff L. C. Walsh. He knew the hardened, realistic old sheriff wasn't anything a hunted man dare minimise.

He rode all one night and made Dead Water, where he'd gunned-down his brother, just at sun-up. The place was wild, isolated, and rank-smelling from the brackish alkali water-hole it derived its name from. Also, it was a boulder-strewn wilderness shunned by man and animal alike. If there was a safe base of operations, Dead Water was it.

He hobbled his horse and stalked over the ground where he and Dell Forrest had run into Jay's ambush. There were little scars on some of the big, smooth old rocks, lighter by shades, where bullets had chipped them. There were black, burnt bloodstains, too. Much more where Dell had died than where Jay had gone over backwards and Mort had taken one horrified, unbelieving look at his brother and fled from the unnerving sight.

It was a bleak spot, but Mort's conditioning was proof against it. He couldn't absorb nor exude any more misery. He was drained dry of the stuff and filled to the brim with it at the same time.

An outlaw was appropriately termed "Owlhooter." He rode in the protective folds of the secret night. His call was the common one of night owls. Mort embraced the new role with no eagerness but with considerable talent. He slept during the days as best he could, with perspiration running in rivulets off him, and rode at night. He watched Sheriff Walsh take out two posses from Clearwater and come back with them, in his trips over the wastelands. He could imagine the curses of the riders just from seeing how they slumped in their saddles on foot-sore horses. Slumped and dehydrated, uncomfortable and empty handed.

And he rode for the Cameron ranch six

days after the last posse had half-heartedly scoured the range for a man most of Clearwater was certain would be far south of the border by that time. Tassie Clement knew better; no one else did.

He rode through the dusk with the full knowledge that, after tonight, with any luck, Clearwater would know he hadn't left the country. He planned to get his payment for Reilly in a blaze of gunfire. After that, he thought, perhaps he'd ride for Mexico; but it was a vague idea. He didn't count much on it, actually. The Camerons were known gunhands.

There was a knife-edged moon that cast about as much light as the inside of a well. Mort rode from experience. There wasn't a foot of Paiute Valley he didn't know. The night seemed to be an ally, too. Then, somewhere up ahead, around the Cameron's buildings, a horse whinnied shrilly, evidently smelling Mort's animal coming through the oppressive heat. Mort sawed the reins gently to keep his own beast from answering, and swore aloud.

He sat for a long fifteen minutes, just listening. No dog barked, and the unseen horse didn't repeat his call. There were no men-sounds, either. He moved forward again, but warily now. He was thinking of survival only in terms of getting his own job done before he cashed in. Naggingly, in the back of his mind, was a wish to wrench the truth out of one of the men he sought about who actually had killed Pat Reilly, before he launched the Camerons into eternity. It wasn't important, really, for Pat was dead; but he wanted to know anyway, just in case he might have to ride further afield, after men he didn't suspect right then of complicity.

A crooked finger of pine forest made an invading wedge about a half-mile from the Cameron's log-buildings. There were stumps all around the place where men had cut winter wood for many years. Mort rode back into the trees and left his horse and spurs, unshipped his carbine and started back again, afoot. There was no light visible at the cabin, but it was late. Close enough to see the corrals and the barn, he went cautiously. A little warning pricked him when he was close enough to see that no animal except one big stud-horse was in the corral or the barn. The ranch had a deserted, abandoned air to it. He stood behind the stud's corral and studied the yard. It was too dark to see horse sign. He squinted into the night, searching for the door to the massive, squatty log-cabin; but it was too far away. If there was the customary big brass padlock on it. . . . He shook his head irritably. They'd have to be there. If they weren't, he had no idea where to look for them.

Gnawed at by uncertainty, conscious of the deserted atmosphere of the place, he went carefully around the corral searching for a safe route to the house. There was none. No rose arbour or flowering hedge, because no womenfolk lived there. The yard was as bare and functional as most man-run cow outfits were.

He considered the scant forty feet he'd have to cross in the open, and chanced it. The element of surprise lay with Mort Ramsey, or so he thought. He banked heavily on that one. There was the same eerie ghostliness at the Cameron place that his own ranch had been steeped in the night he'd found Pat Reilly dangling from the barn baulk. Mort was up close to the cabin's walls, though, before it struck him. Made the sweat run in ticklish cold drops between his shoulder-blades. Without knowing it, he was attuned to the night. Aware of it now as something sinister, not as an ally to an owlhooter.

Motionless and hunkering, he held his carbine with oilyslick fingers and mentally sniffed for the cause of his abrupt sensation of danger. It was all around him in the darkness. In the almost tangible silence that hung like doom over the place. He listened for night sounds and heard none. The old man's advice came back to him. "When in doubt, son, hide out." Right then, however, he was annoyed by it. This was the end of the trail; no place to hide if he had wanted to. Not without recrossing forty feet of open space, anyway.

He got up and moved without a sound. There was one thing he had to know: whether the door was padlocked or not. Darkly dressed, he was a fluid shadow in a gloomy world of stationary ones. He made it to the corner where the sagging old porch jutted, took a long, uneven breath, and looked around at the door. It wasn't padlocked. Two things to do, then. One, get inside and find the Camerons. Two — kill them.

He was no longer conscious of the warning in the back of his mind. He had a course to follow, and moved up on to the old porch to follow it. Several rickety, handmade chairs, quaintly covered with moth-eaten bear-hides, were carelessly scattered about, as though the Cameron brothers had left in a hurry the last time they had sat out there. Mort glanced once, then ignored them. It was his last mistake of the still night. His first mistake had been crossing the open space between the house and the barn.

"Freeze, Ramsey!"

Mort did, mainly because he couldn't see who had spoken or where the man was.

"Drop it."

Mort inaccurately placed the man around the corner of the house at the far end of the porch. It was impossible to place him exactly by his voice. "Not on your life. Come out into the open. You can have a chance at getting me for your brother. Just step out where I can see you."

"I didn't lose any brother, Ramsey," the hidden man said evenly, unexcitedly, each word as calm and cold as glacier ice. "Now, drop that carbine!"

Mort still hesitated. Puzzled, targetless, he had no choice. The gun made a metallic, dull clatter at his feet.

"Use your left hand an' drop that six-gun."

"Come out into the open," Mort said.

"Sure — as soon as you shuck that pistol. Come on — hurry it up."

It wasn't a Cameron, Mort was certain of that. They would have come shooting and yelling. He would have been dead for minutes, by now. Then who?

"Dump that gun — Ramsey!"

If there was a way out Mort couldn't find it. He obeyed.

"Phew! Damned hot back of these bear-skins."

"Walsh!"

"Yeah." The sheriff stood up. He was slightly taller than Mort Ramsey. A deliberate, shrewd man. As hard and uncompromising as the bailiwick he ruled with scattergun law. Characteristically, he was blunt, frank, and harboured no illusions.

"Been waiting around this tick-trap ranch every night for a damned week, for you to show up. Just about gave you up.

Mort stood in limbo. His objective — the one thing he'd thought about day and night for a week — was gone. He groped in his mind. It couldn't happen like this — but it had. He was a prisoner. Tassie had been right. He blinked and shifted his footing. Stared at the sardonic-looking man with the cocked gun in his fist.

"Dammitall," he said unsteadily.

Walsh nodded. "Me too. Why'd you string up Lem Cameron?"

"For Pat Reilly."

"Yeah; I guessed as much. It wasn't for your brother, it was for Pat."

"Yeah." The shock persisted. It was evident in the smallness of Mort's voice. "Why'd you send me out after my brother, Walsh? That's what caused this whole damned. . . ."

Walsh's gun dipped a little when he interrupted Mort. He put all his weight on one leg and relaxed. "You're jumpin' to conclusions, Ramsey. I didn't know who those stage robbers were. I needed a posse and you came along. If I'd known one of them was your brother, you'd of been the last man on earth I'd want riding behind me when I went after 'em."

Mort looked back at the situation. The only conclusion he came up with was a pretty raw joke played on him by a macabre Fate. He kept staring at the lawman, thinking to himself how ludicrous it was that Tassie Clement had been right after all. Walsh and the law had him. He had never understood the sheriff at all. Just hadn't considered him a threat because he hadn't thought about him, that was all. He'd wanted the Camerons. Everything else had been secondary. Now the Camerons were secondary to his own fate as a wanted man under the gun of a lawman.

"Where are the Camerons?"

"Wouldn't worry about them if I was you,

Ramsey. Where you're going you'll get lots of company just as sorry as they are, and just as ornery."

"You know who lynched Pat Reilly?"

"One at a time, Ramsey. Right now you're the feller that Clearwater's up in arms about. Pat'll be taken care of as soon as I've gotten you cached away." Walsh's unblinking regard didn't waver. "Where's your horse?"

"Up in that clump of trees behind the barn a ways."

The Sheriff nodded slightly, speculatively. "You have a bootleg gun?"

"No."

"I could make you strip, Ramsey."

"I don't have."

"Your word?"

"Yes."

Walsh stood silent for a moment. "All right. I'll be behind you on the way into town, anyway. Walk down by the corral: I left my stud-horse there. My gear's in the barn. You'll saddle up for me, then we'll go up an' fetch your horse. Let's go."

Mort's chagrin had passed. He was boiling with disgust at himself. The sheriff stood out in the open, beyond arms' reach, and supervised the catching and saddling of his stallion.

"Let you in a little secret of mine, Ramsey. Know how I was ready for you when you showed up?"

"No." Mort slammed down the blanket and saddle, worried up the latigo — shoved his fist between the horses side and the leather — and cinched it up. The big horse grunted and switched his tail once, resentfully.

"Don't cut him in two, dammit. Well, anyway, whenever I plan a night ambush I ride that stud-horse. He'll smell out a strange critter and nicker, like he did when he smelled you riding in. After that all I got to do is wait."

Mort pulled his fist loose and made a cold smile. "Pretty good, Sheriff; I'll remember that. Here y'are." He held out the reins. Walsh motioned him out into the yard with his gun-barrel. Mort obeyed quickly, moving so as to get as many feet between himself and the lawman as he could, before the sheriff toed into the stirrup, grunted, and heaved himself upwards. But he never made the horse's back. His own rather considerable weight was far too much for the slack latigo and cincha. He swore in sudden understanding even as the horse shied violently and the saddle slipped. Mort watched, holding his breath; saw the catastrophe in the making; then ran as hard as he had ever run in his life. He was beyond the barn and the corrals and sucking air into his lungs in gulps when he heard the stud-horse's last frightened snort. He didn't look back. Didn't have to. With the cincha hanging loose after he'd extricated his fist, Sheriff Walsh's weight had done the rest. Caused the lawman to be thrown violently when the startled horse jumped the first time. Distantly Mort heard the livid pro-fanity that shattered the dark silence.

Reaching his own animal, Mort didn't bother to tug-up his own cincha when he vaulted into the saddle, whirled, and spurred wildly in among the deep gloom of the forest. His heart was beating with un-steady intensity, the breath came short and his lungs felt like they were raw. He rode recklessly, dodging when he could and leaving most of it up to his horse. He could hear Walsh coming in behind him, and not far off, either. His bid for freedom had been a calculated one based on desperation. That it had worked surprised him more than it pleased him, but there had been no other way out. In Walsh's eyes he was a murderer; in the eyes of Clearwater he was lynch-bait. Either way he would have lost except for the mad gamble, that had worked.

Unarmed now and known to be in the country, Mort's failure was more serious than he knew at the time. He slackened the killing pace only when he no longer heard the sheriff behind him, and after that he wandered in the forest until just before dawn, then stopped and awaited daylight. The trees, he knew, were part of an overall breadth of land known as "the primitive area." Uncharted and uninhabited since the Indians had been rounded up and shipped to the Territory.

With the first blush of new day, Mort rode out on a slope and took his bearings. Below and eastwards, in a grassy clearing, was a ranch. He rode towards it openly. Unarmed, he had no choice. In the ranch-yard a gaunt old wolfhound growled ominously but made no move towards following up his disapproval. Mort tied up and hallo'ed the house. There was no response. Crossing the yard, and conscious of the savage heat in the breathless little valley, he stepped up on to the porch and thumped on the door.

"Come in." It sounded feeble and muffled.

Wondering, Mort pushed inside, stood beside the door waiting for his eyes to become adjusted to the cool, dark interior, and smelled an odour that made him wince.

"Who's that? You, Sam? Come over here by the cot, will you?"

Mort went, forgetting his own predicament for the moment. An old man lay, unshaven and filthy, feverish-faced and barely rational, blinking moistly up at him.

"You ain't Sam. Who are you?"

"Never mind that," Mort said. "What's wrong here?"

"Sickness, boy. Been flat f'three days. Can't get up. Got critters in the corral. Dog ain't been fed, either. Got to have some help, stranger — got to."

"Sure," Mort said. "You have any whisky?"

"In the cupboard over the cookstove. Over — there."

Mort got it, poured a dipper half-full and took it back to the sick man, hoisted him up and poured some of it down him, more of it over him. "When'd you eat last, old-timer?"

The oldster shuddered and lay back. Colour came into his face, but splotchily. "Don't recollect. Turn out them cows in the corral, will you? Horse in the barn, too. An' the dog — ain't been fed in three days."

Mort nodded, straightened up and went back outside. He deliberately left the door open. The sunlight and fresh air hit him twin sledge-hammer blows that were welcome after the foetidness of the cabin.

The old man's animals were in bad shape. It took almost an hour of careful handling before they could be turned loose to drink and graze. The dog hadn't suffered nearly as much, indicating there were ample small animals he could catch in his need, but Mort fed him well anyway. Finally, when, it was all done, Mort straightened up and shook off the annoying sweat, studied the secluded little valley, then went back inside. The room had aired out a lot. He saw the beads of unhealthy perspiration on the old man's face, and worried.

"What kind of sickness do you have, pardner — you know?" A weak head-shake was his answer. "Gimme another sip of whisky, will you, stranger?"

"Sure, after you eat."

There was a sense of selflessness, almost peacefulness, in what Mort did for three hours, then. It wasn't until he saw the pistol in the shiny old holster that he remembered his purpose in coming to the ranch in the first place. The old man lay with only his eyes moving when Mort took the gun down, shucked its greenish loads and replaced them from his own shell-belt, and dropped the weapon into his own empty holster. Neither of them said a word until Mort had remade the oldster's bed, washed him vigorously, and fed him. Then the watering old eyes, steady and showing much less of their former fever, regarded Mort with an unblinking shrewdness.

"There's a carbine in the corner back of the stove. Feller likes to have both, when he's riding. I always do."

Mort looked around into the old eyes, read nothing there, and nodded. "Thanks. I'll borrow it for a while, too, if you don't mind."

"Hell; keep 'em. I owe you more'n that."

"You don't owe me a damned thing. Just lucky I came along. You have any kin? Wife — or kids — or someone who can come up here and watch out for you until you're back on your feet?"

"No woman, son; never could tolerate the tomfool things. Got a brother, though. If you're heading towards Clearwater you might let him know I'm bed-bound, if y'would."

"Sure," Mort said uncertainly. "Where'll I find him?"

"Ask around for Sheriff L. C. Walsh. That's him."

Mort was turning away when the old-timer spoke. If the shock showed he was certain the old man hadn't seen it. But the silence was eloquent to a man who had lived as long as this cowman. His reedy voice even had a tincture of genuine amusement in it when next he spoke.

" 'Course, you don't have to ride in an' tell my brother. Y'could send him word, maybe. Give some kid a nickel an' write a note."

Mort turned then, saw the half-concealed, wry humour in the seamed face, and smiled. "Reckon I could at that," he said. "Well — I'll do what I can, pardner. Got to be moving along now. Don't worry, I'll find help and send someone back, anyway."

He rode down across the little valley reluctantly. A man with no purpose now, being blown by a destiny he had come to distrust; but at least he was still free, and armed again. Raising his brooding glance to the jumble of hills and mountains around him, he thought of the Camerons and the old man whose gun he'd taken. He'd ride first to Clearwater and send a message to the sheriff. After that he'd put an ear to the ground; try to ferret-out where the Cameron brothers were, and hunt them down.

The ride took up all that remained of the day because he dared not use known trails over the wilderness road he travelled across the primitive area, and at the outskirts of Clearwater in the dusk he reined up and looked at the town. If ever a man was putting his head into the lion's mouth, it was Morton Ramsey. He shrugged and made a cigarette, sat there smoking and thinking.

Clearwater loomed like a series of finger-stumps against the late evening. A few yellow-orange splashes of lantern light spilled down into the dusty, weathered lull of the place. It was supper-time for townsmen.

The village was a trail town that had come to life out of necessity and stayed alive for the same reason. It was utilitarian only; ugly and blocky and garish, with the needs of stockmen in its stores and railroad chutes, and with none of the requirements of a settled, permanent community at all. Like a garbage dump, for instance, or civic spirit. They might come some day, but until they did Clearwater would continue to grow fat, blue-bellied flies, and renegades by the score. Clearwater was a shipping terminus for cowmen and a roistering-place for the riders, and a way-station for all kinds of overland travellers. Aside from that it wasn't anything much, unless being the headquarters for the Big Sink Stage Company lent it quasi-respectability — for stage lines were big business.

Mort thought of the stage line. It had been the cause — if not the reason — for Jay Ramsey's death. Indirectly, too, it was responsible for the death of Lem Cameron and Pat Reilly.

A few men lounged around the livery barn, but Mort had no intention of going up to them. There wasn't a kid in sight. He squirmed irritably in the saddle — and suddenly thought of Tassie Clement. There was his way out, and it was the least risky thing he could do.

Riding around the town so as to enter the alleyway behind the Clement house, Mort found that the very thing he had been annoyed about before was actually a blessing. Suppertime for the townsmen made it possible for him to tie up at the Clement back gate without meeting a single soul. His spurs rang musically when he approached the back door and knocked on it. He was back in the shadows when the young boy came out, peering up at him.

"Tassie here?"

"Yeah; I'll fetch her."

Mort breathed easier when the girl came out, hesitated once when she saw him silhouetted, then moved swiftly, jerkily, over beside him.

"What are you doing here? Mort — you're utterly foolish."

He watched the way the weak light played over her upturned, pretty face, and made his voice deliberately harsh. "I didn't come here to pay a social call, ma'am. Sheriff Walsh's got a brother lives back in the hills. He's sicker'n the devil. I came to get you to go tell the sheriff."

"Is that all you came for?"

"Yes. Now who's being foolish? What else'd bring me?"

"Jay and the Camerons."

"Jay?" Mort said in mild surprise. "Bury him where you want to. I don't care what you do with him. Not now." He blinked twice at her. "The Camerons? What about them, Tassie?"

"Mort: haven't you heard?"

"Heard what?"

"Jay isn't dead."

"WHAT?"

"He isn't. You shot him along the side of the head. Most of one ear is gone and there's an ugly groove. I saw the sheriff this morning. He told me."

"Tassie —" He closed his mouth over words of protest and stared down at her. "I don't believe it. I saw him fall. Took a look at him when I went by. There was blood over his shirt-front. It made me sick. He was sprawled out in the rocks. I — got on my horse and rode — off." His voice trailed off and his stare continued.

Tassie was holding one set of fingers tightly within a circlet of her other hand, looking at his face. "But he wasn't dead, Mott. Sheriff Walsh said he wanted you as a witness for the killing of Dell Forrest. They're going to try Jay for murder as soon as he's able to move around a little. He's in town here, but he isn't dead. Mort — what I started to tell you is that Walsh has both the Cameron brothers in jail, here in Clearwater."

Mort's astonishment was complete, "Walsh has 'em in jail?" She nodded, and his glance slid off her face. "I'll be damned."

"What's wrong with that, Mort?"

"Pat Reilly got lynched because the Clearwater friends of the Camerons thought I'd killed my own brother, who was one of the gang. Now it turns out I didn't kill Jay after all, but I did kill Lem Cameron over Pat, and the whole doggoned thing started over Jay — who isn't dead after all." He glanced at her swiftly and made a dry, brittle little laugh.

"And you know what, Tassie? Mort Ramsey's the only one of the lot who's really guilty of murder now, except for whoever strung Pat up."

"No," she said quickly. "Jay's a murderer —"

"Go ahead and say it: Jay's a murderer, too." He waited for her to speak, to deny she was about to say it that way, but she didn't make a sound. "So, Tassie, I'm the outlaw; and it's kind of funny, isn't it?"

"You mean ironic, Mort; but it isn't funny at all."

"Jay's alive and the Camerons are in jail and Mort Ramsey — the killer — is still at large." He pulled his mouth downwards as though to give that mirthless chuckle again, but she stopped him.

"Mort — stop it. I'll go tell Sheriff Walsh about his brother. Will you go with me?"

"You're a kid, Tassie."

"What do you mean?"

"He'd throw down on me before I could get through the door. Any trial I'd get in Clearwater would get me hung before breakfast."

"But, Mort: you've got to give up. They'll keep on hunting you from now on. Sheriff Walsh is a manhunter. That's his business. He's already gotten everyone who's mixed up in this mess. He'll get you, too."

Mort shrugged. "Maybe. Maybe not.

Right now all I'm interested in is that Walsh's brother gets some help — and what to do next."

"Then give yourself up, Mort. You can't win, believe me."

Mort ignored her words. "The Camerons're locked up, so I don't reckon I can get at them, or — say — are you going over to tell Walsh about his brother right now?"

"Should I?"

"Yes. The old man's about dead. Well — he *was* almost dead, anyway."

Tassie nodded her head once, brusquely. "I'll go. He'll be at home now. It's suppertime. Have you eaten, Mort?"

"Sure," he lied. "Don't worry about me."

"I can't help it, Mort. I — just can't."

"You don't have to tell Walsh *I* told you his brother's sick, do you?"

"I suppose not. Mort?"

"Yes? Say — what's wrong with you?"

"Jay told the sheriff he's going to hunt you down and kill you if he gets out of this trouble."

Mort made a wry face. "He's got about as much chance of getting out of that old lawdog's hands as I have of flying. Besides, Jay wouldn't stand a chance against a man who knew he was coming after him."

"But you might not know, Mort."

"I'll know all right, Tassie; don't worry about that. Until Grat and Davis Cameron're dangling from a tree-limb, and Jay's up there beside them, I'll keep on using the eyes in the back of my head. Don't worry yourself, Tassie; not about me."

"That's all I do," she blurted out swiftly. "Worry, worry, worry!"

He was jarred by the way she said it, close to hysteria, with her eyes wide and brimming. "Well — for — Tassie!" The dumb shock wore thin enough for him to vaguely understand and stare at her.

"Oh!" she said abruptly. "You're — you're impossible, Mort Ramsey; just impossible. Why won't you try and get yourself out of this mess? Can't you see there'll be only one ending to things, the way they're going now?"

Nettled, and bewildered, too, he frowned down at her, "Just how can a murderer climb out from under his crime? You tell me and I'll do it."

"Give yourself up. Go see —"

"That's ridiculous, girl. Plumb ridiculous."

She looked as though she would slap him. Her head jerked up and her eyes blazed out at him. "Damn you!" she said suddenly.

"You're more than a fool — you're blind, too." Then she swung one small hand so quickly he hardly saw it moving until the sting of the blow across his face made him blink.

Moving automatically, he caught her arm and held it. The anger of moments before was gone in his astonishment. Shaken, they stood like that for seconds, then she tugged.

"Let me go!"

He didn't speak at all. Her face was flushed with a luminous beauty that the night enhanced. Even the uneven, throbbing pulse in the V of her neck was suddenly visible to him. He reached down and got her other arm, pulled her in against him and very deliberately brought his head down. Tassie didn't resist, but she didn't respond, either. It was as though a sudden chill had seized her. She was rigid until his mouth covered her own, then a quiver went through her. Mort let her go finally, but she didn't break away until his head was moving, brushing hard, chapped lips across her mouth the second time, then she turned her head just a trifle.

"Why did you do that?"

He watched her take two short steps backwards, and answered stupidly but honestly:

"I don't rightly know, Tassie. You'd — best go now."

"And you?"

"I'll go, too."

"Where?"

"What's the difference?"

"How can you say that, Morton Ramsey?"

He understood her meaning and the way she felt about it, oddly enough. "Well — I've got to keep moving." He drew in a long, noisy breath and exhaled it slowly. "Tassie — I'm sorry. I didn't think when I — when we — did that. It — just seemed natural, right then."

"I know, Mort. The most natural thing under the sun." She swung away from him but he caught her by the shoulder.

"Don't be sarcastic, girl. You're only making it harder for me to get untangled, kind of."

"And what about me? Would you like to know something, Mort? You wondered why I worried. I'll tell you: because I couldn't help it. It's just natural for me to worry about you. That's natural, then, and there's a reason for it; but, like I said, you're blind. Too blind, maybe. Well — the kiss was natural then, wasn't it?"

That time she whirled and ran towards

the house, and he made no move to stop her. It didn't make sense, what she'd said. Didn't make sense at all; or did it, in some devious, womanly way? He turned and ambled slowly back to his horse, swung up and reined down the alleyway, lost in thought. He'd had an idea back in the Clement's back-yard, but that had been before he kissed Tassie. Now, he had trouble getting his mind to function right again.

It took nearly five minutes of effort to shake off the peculiar sense of depression that enveloped him, and all the time there was the vivid memory of Tassie's kiss on his mouth to disturb him. And — Jay wasn't dead. That had staggered him. He had seen dead men before. Now he wondered uncomfortably just how many hadn't actually been dead after all. He'd never stayed around any of them to find out.

Up until now, Mort Ramsey had steered clear of violence unless it couldn't be avoided. But, dead or alive, Jay didn't worry him. Even if he managed to escape, which Mort doubted he'd be able to do, knowing first-hand how Sheriff Walsh worked, it still didn't trouble him. He had an abiding contempt for the rabid, undisciplined, gun-crazy younger brother an unkind fate had saddled him with; but no fear whatsoever.

That wasn't what made him tie his horse just beyond town, under a half-dead cotton-wood tree, and walk across the back alleys afoot. Jay wasn't even in his mind then. As far as Mort was concerned, Jay was as good as sentenced to die for Dell Forrest's killing. And it suited Mort just that way, exactly.

It was the Cameron brothers he wanted now, and they were in L. C. Walsh's strap-steel cages in the stifling little adobe room behind the sheriff's office. And Walsh would be at supper now, like the rest of Clearwater.

The late evening was a long time dying. Late dusk hung on with stubborn tenacity. The smell of curing grass and baked earth was heavy in the night air. If anything, the forepart of the night was hotter than during the day. All the stored-up, reflected heat seemed to find a release when the sun was gone, and ricocheted from the ground up-wards.

Mort was damp with nervous perspiration as well as heat-inspired clamminess. Townsmen were stirring a little. Distantly, the sound of a dog-fight came to him; the added racket of two men whooping at the animals; and some woman, closer, calling a son to late supper. He listened, identifying

70

each sound, cataloguing it for personal import, and wondered how he'd get the Camerons out of their cell, on to horses and out of town, or whether he'd even get the chance. He had no plan beyond getting into Walsh's office. Except for the slim chance that the sheriff wasn't there, Mort was gambling like he had at the Cameron ranch a few days before. But he didn't know it. Didn't think about it at all.

He had no idea at all how slim his chances were. Not until he was coming around the edge of the hay- and grain-shed that adjoined the livery barn and saw the number of people out strolling after supper, snatching a moment of relief from the murderous daylight sunblast.

He wouldn't give up even then, though. That singleness of purpose was still damaging his normally sound judgment. It would continue to do so for a short time yet. He kept his head down to avoid recognition — which wasn't too likely, anyway, as dark as it was becoming — and stalked up the duckboards to Walsh's office. He was in front of a little trash-littered walkway, barely wide enough for a man to walk through, that separated the sheriff's office from a beanery, when he was abruptly disillusioned. The voice wasn't loud or particularly edgy, but it very distinctly meant exactly what it said.

"Stop and don't move, Ramsey. Don't take another step!"

Mort was caught in mid-stride and unprepared. He stopped in astonishment more than obedience. A flicker of movement at the corner of his vision showed him where the person was. In the stingy walkway between the buildings. Apparently the gun-hand had been in there waiting.

"Turn and walk down this path and don't look back. I'll be right behind you."

Mort turned, didn't see his captor, but heard the footbeats as the person edged out around him, shoved the unmistakable barrel of a six-gun into his back and nudged him into the dark maw of the little walkway.

He went, if not willingly, at least briskly. Mort had more to lose by resisting than he had by not resisting. A fight would bring a crowd, the one thing he absolutely did not want. This way, at least, he was still unknown to the angry populace.

Emerging into the refuse-laden alleyway behind Clearwater's Front Street, Mort paused, waiting. The gun touched him gently again, indicating he was to move to the left.

"Over against the jailhouse wall. Back up to it."

He did, then watched the white blouse materialise from behind him; move out and stand where he could get a good, long look.

"Tassie!"

The girl's eyes were bright with excitement. She made a small face at him. "Lord! And you think you're invincible. This makes the second time." Her head wagged a little in obvious wonder at him. It made his colour come up. Humiliated, he could have sworn at her, but he didn't.

"Dear, you're no match for Walsh. He'll get you just like I told you he will. Just like he got the others. At least *they* used their heads. You called me a fool — remember? Not once, but twice. Well, I think you're the fool, Mort." She uncocked the big six-gun and pushed it down the front of her skirt.

"Did you think I was really so childish I couldn't guess what you were thinking, back in the yard? You're so — so naïve, Mort."

"Cut it out," he growled at her. "Why'd you do this?"

"Because, Mister Owlhooter, the sheriff has three shot gun deputies sitting inside that office just waiting for you to open the front door, that's why. Also — because I don't think you're smart enough to get away with a thing like breaking the Camerons out of jail so that you can hang them to a tree-limb somewhere. And — Mort — please," Her voice changed swiftly, the hardness and triumph went out of it in a rush. "Please — don't make things any worse than they are."

He regarded her steadily, unblinkingly, then sighed. "I've been dumb all right. Dumb as hell. Funny it'd be a tyke like you that'd show me how dumb I really was, isn't it?"

"Yes," she said, "very funny. I'm not a tyke, either. I'm big enough to out-think you. Have every time we've met — haven't I?"

"Well —"

"Oh, be masculine, then; don't admit you can ever be wrong."

He admitted nothing, but he pushed off the wall and moved lazily towards her. The closer he got, the larger her eyes became. She had the appearance of a girl on the verge of flight, only she didn't flee. He took her by the shoulders and pulled gently.

"This," he said gravely, "is for scaring the hell out of me."

When his head came down she turned her face away. The scent of her hair was like a breath of late spring. "No, Mort. You can't kiss me and say it's a punishment." She struggled in his grip. "If that's what it was — in the back-yard — I don't —"

"Come here!" He pulled her in closer, roughly. Her resistance crumpled. "I'm kissing you because I — want to — I — reckon."

She looked at him glassy-eyed. "Do you actually know why you're kissing me?"

"No, I don't; but I sure want to." And he did. Held it for a long, indrawn breath, too; then released her, and was only half as horrified as he'd been before. " 'Bye, Tassie. I'll remember this lesson, believe me."

"What lesson? Where are you going?" Her voice was a little higher than usual, and scratchy.

"Back to Dead Water. I've got a camp there. The lesson? I meant about walking in front of places where someone might be hiding." He took five big steps and was lost in the night. She stood still, hearing him go and biting her underlip fiercely.

CHAPTER THREE

Treachery

Mort's camp at Dead Water wasn't the same, though. There was an unfathomable restlessness in him. An irritability that surprised even him. He chalked it up to his inability to avenge Pat Reilly — and knew that wasn't right, either.

The reason was Tassie and two kisses. The hurt within him that was vivid memories of a girl who was the daughter of an executive of the Big Sink Stage Company. A slip of a full-bodied girl who could set a man's soul on fire — and had.

He lay over an entire day, perspiring and thinking. If the Camerons were out of reach, Pat would go unavenged. It was unthinkable. Until last night Mort had felt no especial desire to live; hadn't cared one way or the other. Now, he didn't want to die, but he still had a blood-debt to pay. It never occurred to him that maybe old Pat wouldn't have wanted the Camerons gunned down for vengeance.

And there were the constant thoughts of

Tassie Clement, too. They warped and coloured his thoughts; but at least — because of the inspired longing he now had to go on living — he wasn't thinking blind any more. Her influence was good for him — and he didn't know that, either.

So, before dusk, he got astride and rode in a big, sagging circle out over the uninhabited wasteland, just thinking. It was when he went carelessly up a slight eminence, seeking coolness, that the vapours of indecision and confusion inside him evaporated. There, far away but coming up fast, was a tell-tale dust banner. Symbol of riding men beneath it. Too much commotion for one man — or one girl. The age-old warning to watchers in the desert countries. A sinister dustbanner.

Mort sat there a long time with a sickening thought growing with every forward movement of what was patently a large and heavily armed posse. Tassie. It had to be. No one else knew where he was. He tried to tell himself they had tracked him, but it didn't make sense. Not over ground like rock; not around Dead Water country, which he had chosen particularly because it *was* a trackless wilderness. No; if that was Walsh and a posse, the sheriff could have gotten his information only one way.

Mort's terrible disappointment fed on something else. Why had Walsh staked out the Cameron ranch for a week? Not just because he was hopeful that Morton Ramsey hadn't left the country like everyone else thought he had. But because he *knew* Mort was still in the Valley. Knew it because someone must have told him so — and only one person knew he had decided not to flee after all. Tassie again.

His eyes were pinpointed on the riders. There were eight of them. He could make them out easily enough now. Could see the fading light of a spent day glancing off gunhardware and riding-equipment. It was a posse all right. Riders wouldn't come across a rock jumble like Dead Water in a long lope, in a direct line, unless they had a purpose and a destination.

He turned and rode down off the far side of the little hill, lifted his horse into a lope, and held west by north. He rode with a slow agony of wrath building up inside him. Two kisses for confidence — and treachery. Abruptly he recalled how close he'd been to the sheriff's office, and how Tassie had held him under her gun — then let him walk away. It was a straw that he grasped at eagerly, like a drowning man would, but it didn't bolster him long. She'd had some devious reason for letting him go that time. Must have had. If not, then why did she turn right around and stick the law on him; betray him like she had, now?

He rode until the distance was sufficient to make his capture almost impossible; then, in a surge of the old savagery, swung his horse south and held him to a gruelling gait until he was back on the outskirts of Clearwater again. He had an anger- and revenge-inspired idea. Revenge for Pat and a sardonic repayment for Tassie as well. A fool? Maybe; but he was thinking that at least two people wouldn't think so by sun-up. Not if he was a good enough actor, anyway.

Leaving his horse tied to a stud-ring half-buried in an ancient cottonwood tree at the edge of town, Mort went down the back alley to the Clement's back gate and passed through, brooding-eyed and vicious looking. When he knocked this time, Tassie herself answered, as though she had been close and waiting.

"Mort!"

He heard the way she said his name, like it was air being pumped out of her. Kept a perfectly straight face until she had come out into the cool evening and was beside him — then he smiled at her. Made it a dazzlingly charming smile, that showed his even white teeth in the tawny swarthiness of his copper-coloured face.

"Came back for another kiss, Tassie."

"Oh, Mort!" She said it with an effort to control the frantic, desperate fear that showed in her eyes. "Why are you so completely reckless?"

"For you. There's no other reason under the sun — any more. Just you, Tassie."

He touched her. Felt the firmness and warmth of her. Caught a scent of the tantalising odour in her hair. Took her in his arms and kissed her, then didn't let her go but kissed her again and said things he would have never been capable of saying, except for that acid core of sickening despair and terrible hurt within him. Made ardent, abandoned love to her there in the deep, quiet night, with the smell of the rangeland and town flowerbeds around them. Using the bitter hatred that was in his breast as a spark for his inspiration of deceit.

And Tassie responded because she was afflicted with the danger to him of staying in Clearwater, as well as the monumental hunger she'd felt for so long for Jay Ramsey's older brother. When he told her he loved her and sealed it with a burning kiss, she responded in silence, not daring to speak.

Only once did Mort feel a terrible, shocked second of guilt. That was when the salty taste of Tassie's silent tears marred an embrace. Burnt his mouth like acid; made him see himself for what he was — what he was doing — for a fleeting second. Then he closed his eyes and refused to look again. It wasn't hard to repay her supposed treachery in kind. Not when he remembered it was his life she had sought to betray.

The night whipped by like a banner in a high wind. Hours tumbling over one another until Tassie begged him to go away. To Mexico, to California, to Arizona, anywhere, and write to her so that she could come to him.

He refused. "Not until I've squared up for Pat, honey."

"Oh, Mort — you can't. God in Heaven, Mort! You'll be killed if you even go near that jail. L.C. is angry about how you escaped him at the Cameron place. Oh, darling — please — oh, please! We've got a right to live and be happy, too, Mort. Don't throw it away over the Camerons."

"Tassie — Pat was more to me than anyone I've ever known. I'd be a pretty low-down critter if I didn't even up for him."

"But Mort," she said in desperation, "you can't get near them. That's exactly what L.C. is using them for. Bait. He knows you want them badly enough to —"

"And I'll get 'em, too, honey."

She sat up in horror, staring at him. Seeing the handsome dishevelled look of him; the way his hair-waves had been pressed down close around the well-shaped head by his hat. How his forehead was five shades lighter than the lower part of his face, protected from the sun by his hatbrim. And it made her strangely uneasy — almost uncomfortable — when she looked over into his eyes and saw the brooding, indefinable look there that was something she couldn't name but could feel cut into her like a sharp knife. He couldn't be shaken from his mad, lethal determination to walk into Walsh's trap and kill the Camerons. And he would probably be riddled before he could get his gun unlimbered.

The awful tragedy of his blindness made her frantic with fear. Love could come like that — and be snatched away just as fast. She shook her head to clear the foggy picture of him before her vision.

"Mort — would you trade them for me? I mean — give me a chance. I'll make you forget them."

He bent forward and kissed her feverishly. The sardonic smile was back, in the soft, eerie light. It matched the cougar look in his eyes. Tawny and triumphant. "It just isn't a trade, Tassie. First, the Camerons for Pat; second, you for life."

"There won't be any!" She glared at him. "There won't be any life for us, Mort. They'll —"

"Kill me. All right, darling. It's a matter of — well — honour, to me — would be to any man. You wouldn't marry a coward, or a man who wouldn't —"

"Yes I would. Don't fool yourself. If you are a coward, then I love 'em."

"Well," he said distantly, "I'm not."

Tassie smoothed out her blouse and ran a numb hand through her thick mass of short hair before she answered him. She had an idea. Studied the ground in front of them, turning it over in her mind. If she'd seen the intent look on Mort's face. . . . But she didn't.

"Then I'll be an outlaw, too."

"What are you talking about?" Mort said it hopefully, seeing his plan maturing; knowing he'd succeeded — or hoping desperately he had.

"I can get the Camerons loose."

"Tassie! You're talking like a kid."

"Am I? I can get L.C.'s guards out of there and turn both the Camerons loose in fifteen minutes."

"How?" He challenged her, hardly breathing.

She didn't look at him as she spoke. "I've been in to see L.C. almost every day since you — since this thing broke. His deputies know me. In fact, I took them over an apple pie, day before yesterday. I can get them outside, easily. Tell them L.C. wants them down by the livery barn. They'll go. After all, I'm the daughter of the vice-president of the company that was robbed. They'll —"

"But how'll you get the Camerons out of their cells?"

"I've seen L.C.'s padlock key a hundred times. It's in the top drawer of his —"

"Will you do this, Tassie?" He was fervently in earnest now, but she was too upset to notice. "It's — well — sort of treacherous, honey."

She looked at him. The glance was an eloquently silent rebuke, and a mirrored hopelessness that she had no choice at all. Morton Ramsey was more to her than anything in life. Even her own reputation; her honour, or just anything at all.

"Treachery, Mort? A woman in love will do anything to protect the man she loves."

"I reckon," he said drily, getting up and dusting off his knees so that she wouldn't see the sheen of triumph in his eyes.

Standing, Tassie had an awful moment of clarity. The thing she had said she'd do looked enormous. She reached over and clutched Mort. "Mort — I'm scared silly."

He kissed her very gently while he held her close. "Just turn 'em loose, honey, then get out of that office. They'll find their guns in Walsh's desk and take out of there like fresh-cut calves. Don't you be anywhere near. I owe you a lot, but not a bullet."

"That was a funny thing to say, Mort."

He laughed, pushed her out to arms' length, and looked down at her. "You have the nerve, Tassie?" Before she could answer he shook her gently, still smiling. "As soon as I settle, I'll let you know where I am, darling."

One more kiss and he was gone, leaving Tassie with her mounting apprehension. She peered into the night for him, remembering then that she hadn't asked him what he intended to do, or how he'd do it.

Mort went back to his horse and mounted. He rode into town brazenly enough, taking the one unavoidable risk of recognition there was no way to avoid, then he sat in his saddle like a silhouetted statue and waited.

The minutes went along in a shackled drag that seemed like hours and days and lifetimes to him. He palmed his hand-gun and held it cocked in his lap. Strollers were passing. Occasionally they would toss a careless glance as they passed. If any thought it strange that a man would sit on his horse at a hitchrack, none gave any sign of it.

The sweat ran along his ribs beneath his shirt and annoyed him. The ebb and flow of pedestrian traffic in front of Walsh's office never seemed to break while someone entered. In fact, Tassie had already performed her part of the pact, although Mort didn't know it; hadn't seen her hurry up-town and play her part so well that both deputies had gone trooping down to the livery barn without a suspicious glance at her.

He was startled, then, when two men emerged abruptly from the sheriff's office and hurried out into the roadway, stood a second, then made a bee-line for the hitchrack, in front of a garishly lighted and noisy saloon. He watched, wondering if the two men were the deputies; and, by the time it dawned on him they weren't, the Camerons were both mounted and flogging their way in a thunderous, bellydown run out of Clearwater.

He raised his six-gun as the wild riders exploded northwards through town. He heard a man's furious oath and angry shout as the brothers swept close past the livery barn, and ignored the sounds as he whirled his horse and dug in the hooks, riding after them and not daring to shoot. He saw a swishing, fleeting array of white blobs that were startled faces as he raced past, and ignored them all in his concentration on the dimming shadows ahead. The old singleness of purpose was driving Mort Ramsey again. He was out of town almost as rapidly as the escaping prisoners were, and only once was there the throaty, outraged bellow of a rifle to indicate that at least one of the lawmen had kept his carbine in hand when he'd walked down to meet a sheriff who wasn't waiting at all.

The Camerons saw Mort coming. They had no idea who he was, but the rhythmic beat of horse's hooves echoed in their wake, and that meant they were being pursued. Both of them twisted and fired hand-guns. Mort didn't bother to reply. He waited until Clearwater was a pale orange glow far behind, and the Camerons' stolen horses were racing uphill, their breath rattling soggily past extended nostrils, following the stage-road that ran as straight as an arrow; then he reached forward and tugged out his carbine.

The back of a running horse is the world's worst shooting platform. Mort, like all the old-timers, knew it. He kept the stubby gun athwart his upper legs, just in case, but he didn't bother to answer the wildly inaccurate firing of his prey.

The Camerons cut off the stage-road and cut south-east. Mort followed, squinting into the weakly illuminated night, irritated at the anaemic moon for its lack of co-operation in his chase. Apparently the brothers had a rendezvous spot in mind, for they rode fast and without a shout between them, indicating they had previously agreed on their destination. Mort clung to their trail like a tick, never favouring his horse until he felt the animal falter under him. Then, suddenly frantic with fear that the outlaws would escape after all, he reined up a little and allowed the dripping-wet horse to drop into a smooth lope that ate up the miles with rocking regularity.

The Camerons, too, finally slowed. Pursuit from Clearwater would be hopelessly outdistanced, anyway, and none of the three wanted men would be trackable until sun-up — by which time, Mort felt, Walsh would be welcome to whatever was left.

Mort gained on the brothers easily when the Camerons slowed down. He stopped often to listen, guessed their course from the sounds, and pushed on again. Half smiling, he wondered how the night-riding pair liked being the hunted instead of the hunters. Out of nowhere, and apropos of nothing, he saw the dear vision of Tassie in his mind's eye. The girl's look was one of dry-eyed reproach. Mute injury that writhed like illness was in the background of her glance. He tried to shrug away the picture. Even spoke to it aloud as he rode.

"You asked for it, Tassie. Telling Walsh where I was so's he could get me. If you ever see Mort Ramsey again, girl, he'll be a lot older than he was when he made love to you."

"Bang!"

Mort threw himself sideways off the horse but held on to one of the split reins. Cursing under his breath for giving himself away by speaking out loud, he lay perfectly still, listening. The horses were no longer moving. Good. The Camerons had decided to kill the lone horseman who had trailed them from Clearwater. Mort levered a shell into his carbine and waited.

"What's that, back there?"

Mort didn't answer. His horse was moving sideways, nervously. Another voice called out softly to the first. "You must've plugged him, Grat. There ain't a sound."

"Don't bet on it, Dave." But hope was in the warning. Mort heard it and didn't move. He could skyline the land, but a brush-patch made it impossible for him to see what he was looking for. Horses. The Camerons, would be holding their horses just like Mort was.

"Hell — you got him all right."

"Can you see him?"

"Not exactly, but I can see his damned horse. It's about done for, the way it's standing there, head down."

"T'hell with the horse; where's the man? You reckon that's the sheriff, or a deputy?"

"Ain't the sheriff; he was out somewhere. Probably looking for Ramsey."

The other Cameron exploded suddenly with blistering profanity. "That might be Ramsey back there."

A long, heavy silence; then: "Yeah; might be at that. Ol' Walsh said he was hot after us. Well — I still say you got him."

"I wonder. Dave? See can you creep down there a little. I'll cover you from here."

Another long silence before Davis Cameron answered. "Like hell. *You* go."

Grat swore at his brother. "You're the one says I got him."

The silence grew into a wall of weighted, thick oppressiveness for Mort. He knew one — and possibly both — of the Camerons would be edging back to where they could see his horse against the soft, dark skyline. He pushed himself backwards very carefully, trying to get as far from the jaded animal as he could. As yet he had no very clear idea where the killers were. Their voices placed one south of him a little, near a big patch of sage and ripgut; while the other one — the one Mort felt sure was Grat, the older brother — seemed to be dead ahead, where a land-swell cut off the skyline. But Mort didn't play his hunch either. He crawled backwards as noiselessly as he could, until he was a good eight feet from his horse, then he flattened out again.

The wait wasn't long, although it seemed to be. Mort had no way of knowing which of the brothers he saw first, but the man was less prudent than an outlaw should have been. He was inching towards Mort's horse from the south-east, hips exposed with every move, shoulders bobbing less conspicuously but still visible every once in a while. Mort shoved his carbine out, aligned it, and waited. Guessing, Mort figured the stalking man was Davis Cameron, the one who'd been so sure Grat's shot had downed Mort. There was the imprudent way the man was exposing himself, too. As though he was confident he'd find a dead man beside Mort's horse.

When the second brother didn't materialise, Mort decided he wasn't coming after all. He was in error without knowing it. The crawling man raised up suddenly, to his knees. He was holding not one six-gun but two — both cocked. Mort could see them just as plainly as he could see the man craning, weaving for better vision, and a perfect target. His finger was tightening around the carbine's trigger when the man spoke, in harsh scorn.

"Hell, Grat; he's dead."

The older brother had more discretion. "Can you see him?"

Mort slacked off on the trigger very suddenly. The Cameron he hadn't seen was moving after all, but not from in front where he'd been lying when he fired at Mort, but from behind him.

The sweat popped out anew on Mort's forehead. Davis Cameron might be an impetuous damned fool, but Grat made up for it with his wiliness. He'd made a big arc and was crawling in from the direction Mort wouldn't expect him from — if Mort wasn't dead.

"Naw," Davis called back, "not yet I can't, but I'm standin' up. Can you see me, Grat?"

"Yes, you damned fool," Grat said swiftly. "Get down!"

But Davis Cameron ignored his older brother's advice and made a derisive snort that carried easily to where Mort was watching him, wanting to kill him and yet unable to as long as his flank was exposed to Grat. Davis Cameron was walking coolly towards Mort's horse. He had holstered one of his belt-guns and held the other one carelessly. Mort dared not move. He would have to shortly, but until he had to, he didn't. He watched the younger outlaw go up to his horse, stop suddenly and crouch a little, peering intently around, then drop to one knee with both guns in his hands again.

"Grat? He ain't here."

"I told you, you damned fool. Get —"

"Bang!"

Mort recoiled from the dust-splash of Davis Cameron's bullet and fired back instinctively. He knew what had betrayed him even as he tugged off his shots at Davis. Moonlight, as weak as watered milk, reflecting off the carbine barrel. He levered in another shell and fired at the downed man, saw him jerk in a convulsion; then Mort rolled frantically sideways. None too soon. A spray of gunshots patterned the spot where his muzzle-flash had come from. Dropping the carbine, Mort jerked at his pistol as he rolled, spun and flinched from the out-thrust tongue of livid orange-yellow that lanced the night inches to the left of him. He fired once, twice, and three times; as fast as he could thumb back the dog and depress the trigger.

The gun bucked hard, slamming back into the pad of his thumb like a mule kick. Silence then. Dread and fear elbowing into the drama like unseen trespassers. Mort rolled farther away and lay belly-down, sucking air into his lungs that tasted like creosote. Sweat dripped off the end of his nose and fell against the flinty ground. He reloaded his .45 and went — inches at a time, with long pauses in between — towards the first man he'd fired at.

It took a full hour to make the cautious advance, but when he'd gotten close enough, and saw his antagonist's condition, he sighed. Wasted time or not, this same man would likely be hale and hearty himself but for the recklessness that had presented him to Mort over the sight of Mort's carbine. He was dead; sprawled out on his back and staring with unseeing eyes heavenward. Mort was so sure of it that he leaned over the man, took up his guns, tossed them aside and was turning away when the smallest of noises made him jerk around. The man's gory shirtfront heaved spasmodically. Mort bent far over and watched the eyes. They moved, although obviously vision was almost gone. He reached down, grasped the shirt and gave the man a ruthless shake.

"You hear me, feller?"

Grey eyes that couldn't altogether focus looked up at him.

"Which one of you hung Pat Reilly?"

The face worked weakly with a flash of understanding, then the eyes worked over to Mort's glance and hung up there. Mort shook the dying man harder.

"Which one of you fellers hung that feller in Ramsey's barn?"

The voice when it came was husky but ragged, and inclined to tail off. "Him? Name Reilly? Did'n know."

"For the last time — who strung him up?"

"Me — 'n Grat — 'n Lem. Caught him turnin' horses out. Hung him."

"Why? Dammit — why?"

"He was helpin' — Ramsey. Ramsey —

killed his brother. Jay was — our pardner. That hombre — he wouldn't say — where Ramsey — was. Stood up — an' — an' — cussed us. We —"

But Mort was moving away, with hatred for the Camerons searing his soul. So all three of the Camerons had done it, had they? Well — he'd killed two of them, but there was a third one of those human wolves somewhere behind him. Dead, possibly; but still, he'd make sure.

Grat Cameron was dead all right. He'd stopped one bullet with the top of his head; another with his throat. Mort stood up and looked at him, and made a sound deep in his throat before he went over and caught his horse.

He rode slowly forward, feeling a lot differently than he'd thought he'd feel after exacting full payment, in blood, for Pat Reilly. There was no sense of elation at all. No bleak satisfaction with himself. Just a knowledge that Pat was paid for — avenged now — and the unkind fate that had dogged Mort right from the day he'd caught up with Jay had whimsically allowed Morton Ramsey to live.

He rode into the coolness of pre-dawn with the curious let-down of post-climax holding him tight. He couldn't go back to

Dead Water. Tassie had sold him out. And he'd devised a way to get the Camerons, pay her back for her treachery, and out-smart the wily old sheriff, too. Still there was no satisfaction.

No glory in any of it. For the Camerons he felt neither pity nor hatred. It was the same with Davis and Grat as it had been with the one he'd hung: Lem. Towards the sheriff he'd never had any animosity. That had been a case of surmounting an obstacle. There was nothing personal or rancorous in it either way. He had pitted himself against a professional man-hunter, and won.

And Tassie. The backwash of emotion, like grey languor, rolled over him. He could remember each kiss; each freckle across the saddle of her nose; each glance she'd given him; and they hurt. He thought of how he'd tricked her into helping the Camerons escape. The deceit was many times worse than the triumph and vengeance he'd gotten by using her like that. He felt dirty and old and very, very tired.

Right after sun-up his horse came across a willow-lined little creek with a goodly head of water in it. He hobbled the animal, after a careful look around the wasteland behind him, stripped down and took a chilly bath. The water made his body feel better almost instantly, but the nagging was still in his mind. With clearer vision, though, he thought back to the things Tassie had done. Why had she helped him with the Camerons? Why had she deliberately put herself in a position of aiding and abetting a jailbreak? And why had she told Sheriff Walsh that he was encamped at Dead Water? It didn't make sense. Any way he looked at it, it just didn't make sense. She had willingly helped him and thereby put herself in jeopardy — and yet, on the other hand, she had sold him out to the law once, that he was sure of; and probably twice. Why?

He struck out due east again, riding like a dazed man. Only remembering to look up and watch for strange horsemen every now and then. He was still travelling like that hours later, close to sundown, when he saw the outlines of a village off on his right a few miles. It was a cow-town, as nearly as he could guess, but he couldn't recall ever having ridden so far from home before, and therefore was at a loss to name the place. It looked about like Clearwater — and a hundred others made the same way in the vast, endless void of lands of the West.

He wanted to ride in, but he didn't go near the place until well after sundown.

Caution dictated that course. Later, though, he rode in, stabled his horse and paid for hay and grain. Then he sought out a beanery and ate. Amazed at his own appetite, he tried to remember when he'd eaten last, gave it up and concentrated on what was before him, finished it off with a lot of black coffee; then went back out into the hot evening, sought out a bench in front of a poolroom and dropped down on the thing gratefully and fished around for a tobacco sack he'd lost somewhere — probably while crawling after the Camerons — and relaxed. It was good to feel the slackness in shoulder muscles tight for so long.

" 'Bacco, stranger? Help yourself."

Mort looked quickly at the seamed, square face of the big, bearded man who'd dropped down beside him. Saw the half-closed, perpetually squinted, faded eyes, with their glint of steel behind the puckered eyelids, and took the little sack the man was offering, with a nod. "Much obliged."

"Plumb welcome." The big man shoved his booted feet out luxuriously and sighed. "Cripes, but it's hot!"

"Yeah." Mort lit up and inhaled deeply. It completed the sensation of well-being.

"T'really appreciate it," the bearded man said ponderously, "y'got to be out in it. I got the first leg o' the Clearwater run fer Big Sink Stage Company. Go fourteen miles over that damned alkali until you're as blind as a bat — danged near — then back again. That's when you appreciate it, stranger, believe me."

Mort took a sidling, longer look. The man's profile was hawkish. His nose was large and hooked. It was hard to read much from a face like that. It was almost completely covered by beard. The man might have been a saint or a first class sinner, there was no way to tell.

"Understand Big Sink Line had a hold-up over by Clearwater a few days back."

The stage driver cleared his throat and spat. "Yeah. Funny mess, too. You hear about it?" The puckered, steely eyes studied Mort casually, frankly.

"Hearsay," Mort said.

"Well, sir," the driver said, with apparent pleasure, "I know the driver well who got held up. Known him for years. Him and me used to make the same run down at Yuma. Well — he was caught flat-footed by this scraggly button of a kid — said he couldn't have been more'n eighteen — where his run goes past a clump of manzanita brush." The man began the task of worrying-up a hand-made cigarette.

Mort pictured Jay in his mind. He didn't look his age, at that. Hadn't since he'd looked Mort up in the Clearwater country and moved in with him.

"This button," the stage driver went on, around a mouthful of smoke, "hauled him up with a pair of pistols all slathered over with silver. Reub said the shine off them damned things liked t'have blinded him. Kid had his saddle all fancied-up with silver, too. Regular fancy-dan, he was." The man reached over and tapped Mort's arm significantly. "That's the kind you want to watch like a hawk. Got a reputation to make. Always need a few killings along with their stick-ups."

"I reckon." Darkness came and brought along a wonderful coolness. Mort smoked and listened, fully relaxed for the first time in days. He was a little drowsy, too.

"Kid told Reub to toss down the box. He did it, naturally, then three more of 'em rode up and sat there sayin' nothin', keepin' the stage covered."

"Were they masked?"

"Oh, sure; but Reub's an old hand. He looked every horse an' saddle over real close. Remembered the brands and markings. Anyway — a kid dolled up like that punk was wouldn't be hard to find — silver from hell to breakfast, like a greaser —

101

they'll get him. The others — that's different. Reub said they were old hands. No marks worth remembering. Quiet and steady. Anyway, the law over at Clearwater'll get that kid unless he's run for it. Be easy to identify him, all right."

"Sure would," Mort said with feeling.

"Yeah. Well, they rode off with the box and the next thing we hear at this end is that Walsh — he's sheriff over there — is hot after this kid. Then, by golly, this afternoon a lady come in on the Clearwater stage — dance-hall girl — an' she said there's a rumour over there that Walsh found this kid's brother, took him along on his posse, and this here hombre found that kid and shot him down. Now — don't that beat hell? Imagine a man killin' his own brother! 'Course, it's probably just talk. We don't know for sure one way or t'other, but if it's true, don't that beat all hell?"

"The kid was an outlaw," Mort said doggedly. "Besides, maybe his brother didn't have any choice. Maybe the kid didn't give him —"

"Naw. Folks don't fight their kin like that. Damnedest thing I ever heard of."

"It sure is," said Mort, rising. "Well — much obliged for the smoke, pardner. *Adios*."

"*Adios.*"

He went down the duckboards towards a saloon. The doziness was gone and the sense of loss and loneliness were back worse than ever. With a long, raking glance over the early patrons of the place, he saw none he knew and went on up to the bar.

"Rye?"

"Beer."

"Right."

He looked into the back-bar mirror and was startled at his own hollow-eyed, whisker-stubbled, villainous appearance.

"Dime."

He paid and drank. The beer stung part way down, cutting away the scorch and trail-dust as it went. He had four more. They weren't cold, but they were cooler than he was, and wet. There was no effect, though. He changed over to rye whisky and drank until the jostling crowd became an annoyance; the perspiring faces shiny globes, floating disembodied and close. And when the girl plucked his arm he turned and saw the bearded stage-driver looking over her head at him in quiet amusement.

"Want to dance, cowboy?"

"There's no music," Mort said surlily, "and I'm not a cowboy."

She laughed into his face. "You've had

more than you need, haven't you?"

Mort almost swore at her. It was the amused look on the driver's face that kept him from it. Awfully easy to make a fool of yourself, he said under his breath, when you're like this. Aloud, he grunted and tugged his arm free. But the girl didn't leave. She moved in closer and kept looking at him. Very suddenly she took his hand in her own and pulled him forcibly away from the bar.

"Come on, cowboy — you're going for a walk."

He went with her, conscious of the tight grip she had on his hand. She made straight for the louvred doors. When they were outside the fresh air came down out of the night like a brainwash. He extricated his fingers with no trouble and looked steadily at the girl. She was pretty, young, and very hard-looking. Nothing soft to her, except the body; it was her almost grim look that made him wonder about her.

"Where are we going?"

"Down to that café and get some coffee."

"Why?" He was suddenly uneasy; suspicious.

She tilted her face up to him. There was a mocking grin in her eyes. "Because you remind me of my brother," she said sarcastically.

Mort laughed and felt better at once, then he shrugged. "Let's go."

They drank three cups of coffee under the bored, disinterested glance of the café proprietor before Mort's mind cleared. The café was empty. The girl was holding her cup with both hands and looking at nothing over the rim of it. Mort noticed that her eyes were almost as black as the coffee was.

"Why'd you do this, Miss?"

She shrugged, answering without looking up. "Just felt like it. You need a shave and some clean clothes."

"Yeah; sure do." He looked down self-consciously, then reddened in spite of himself.

"Beer and rye whisky're a poor substitute for facing trouble — sometimes. You know that, cowboy?"

He was nettled a little. "I'm not a cowboy. I told you that."

She shot him a hard glance. "Now tell me you're not in trouble, too."

"You think I'm in trouble, ma'am?" he hedged, watching her face.

This time she looked straight at him and held his glance. "Think it, cowboy? I know it!"

"All right," he said drily. "I am. Up to my ears. Bad trouble."

"There isn't any other kind."

Mort emptied the cup and pushed it aside. "Want another one, ma'am?"

"No. I didn't even want this one. Listen, cowboy — do me a favour, will you?"

"I reckon. What?"

"Go buy some new clothes, get shaved and bathed — then light out of here. Go back where you came from and face it."

"You're a regular grandmother, aren't you? A pretty, young, old grandmother."

She put her coffee cup down very gently. "It probably looks like it all right." She turned the cup half one way, then back, half the other way, using one hand and watching the half-circles very carefully. "This is the first time I've ever done this."

"You like acting the part?"

"No; not especially. In your case I do."

Mort snorted derisively. "Love at first sight, ma'am?"

"Don't be a damned fool. I don't love you and wouldn't if you were the last man on earth."

"Sure not," Mort said bluntly. "Why are you doing this?"

The dark eyes shone in the soft light of the deserted little café. "Because there's a girl who loves you, boy. I happen to know she does."

"The hell you do," Mort said, badly shaken. "How do you know she does — or did?"

"Because I recognised you when you walked into the saloon tonight. Look, cowboy: I was over at Clearwater when that girl turned those outlaws loose. I heard the whole lousy story just before I pulled out and came over here to take this other job. You think a woman'd do a thing like that — disgrace herself and her whole damned family — if she wasn't love-crazy over the man she did it for?"

Mort was stunned. He didn't speak for a long time. They traded stares, with the noises of town night-life echoing off the walls around them.

"Where'd you see me, ma'am?"

"I was in the doorway of the livery barn waiting for the dray-wagon to fetch my luggage last night when you went by like a bullet after those two outlaws. Hell, cowboy — who do you think bumped into that posseman, or deputy — or whatever he was — that shot at you, anyway? Later, this morning, when I'd heard the whole story, I knew you were after them. The rest of it was easy to figure out."

"And you recognised me tonight, in the saloon?"

"Sure. Did you get those — men?"

Mort nodded. "Yes'm. I owed them that —"

She cut in swiftly. "I'm not interested in that. Just in seeing you go back and wiggle out of your mess, or at least get the girl out of it and take her away from that town. She deserves that, and a lot more, from you. Now d'you understand why I got you out of the saloon before you got fighting drunk? You would've. I've seen your kind before. Quiet and broody. Will you go back?"

"And if I don't?" Mort said.

She got up. "Then I'll know you're exactly like two-thirds of the men a woman meets. And I've known a corralful of them like that."

He looked moodily into his empty cup, saying nothing. The dance-hall girl leaned one hip against the counter and ran her glance over his face.

"Whatever she did to you — did you give her a chance to explain why she did it?"

Mort got up and flipped a coin on the counter. His eyes were creased into a long, painful squint. "I only know *what* she did," he said.

"Yeah. Don't bother to tell me, cowboy."

She turned away and started for the door.

Mort went after her; caught her arm when they were both outside again. "I'm wanted for murder in Clearwater."

"I didn't say you had to stick your head in the noose; but at least go back and see her. Take her away with you, if she'll go. But hell, cowboy, give her a chance, anyway."

She swung away from him and he let her go. The blood was pounding in his head. What the dance-hall girl said was partly right. At least Tassie hadn't sold him out altogether. He *did* owe her for helping with the Camerons. He watched the girl disappear into the night, back up towards the saloon, then he turned slowly across the dusty roadway towards the livery barn.

CHAPTER FOUR

Face Down!

Mort rode back towards Clearwater until he came to the willow-lined creek again. There, exhausted and feeling the letdown from his near-drunk, he unsaddled and stretched out on the mat of dry grass at the creek's edge. He slept, unintentionally, until the hot sun roused him, then he caught his horse and went on again. He half-heartedly attributed his revived feeling to the rest he'd had, and not to the knowledge that he was *en route* to redeem himself in Tassie's eyes — and his own.

The feeling within him was an insidious thing that seemed to grow stronger the farther west he went. It was excitement and a deep, roiled sensation he wouldn't have been able to describe but had no trouble feeling within him, at all.

The closer he got to Clearwater the more he thought of Tassie's actions. There was one thing she'd said that was imprinted indelibly in his mind. It was some sort of a key to the things she'd done, he felt sure; and yet it was irreconcilable with her treachery, too.

"Treachery, Mort?" she'd said. "A woman in love will do anything to protect the man she loves."

He said it aloud, twice, and tried to worry some logic out of it. Man-logic. There wasn't any, not when he thought of Walsh and his posse riding hard towards Dead Water after him. Well, he'd go see her. The dance-hall girl had been right. He owed Tassie *that* much. Besides, there was this incomprehensible mystery to the way she had acted. A man wanted to know why people did things. Mort wanted to know why Tassie had given him away, then turned right around and helped him, at her own peril. It didn't make man-sense at all.

Clearwater loomed garishly ahead. He reined up and wagged his head. Morton Ramsey, wanted for the deliberate murder of Lem Cameron, riding into town in broad daylight. It was crazy. He could see the north-south stage road from where he sat. Could even make out the buggy and saddle-back traffic going leisurely over it. And Tassie. . . .

He ran a bronzed hand along the angle of his jaw, felt the stubble there and half-smiled to himself, kicked up his horse and rode recklessly around the town until he was approaching from the south, then he rode in and swung down at the farthest hitchrack. The town was bustling with activity. Mort stood back in the meagre shade of a barber's shop overhang and gazed steadily at the little jailhouse up in the middle of Clearwater, some distance off. The place didn't seem very busy from the outside. He wondered if L.C. was in his office, grinned fiercely at the look he could imagine would spread over those craggy features when Mort walked in and handed over his gun.

First, though, he wanted to clean up, get a shave, some new pants and a shirt — and see Tassie. He went into the deserted barber's-shop, got a mechanical nod from the proprietor, and eased down into the chair.

"Haircut?"

"Yeah. Haircut, shave, and a bath."

The shears snipped a few times in the barber's hand while the barber himself studied Mort's profile guardedly. Sounds of town life came and went intermittently. Mort watched every passer-by; recognised some; wondered if those who glanced up in passing recognised him, and didn't worry much about it. It didn't make much difference. He had made his mind up. All he wanted was an hour-and-a-half of freedom. After that, Walsh could have him. He couldn't prove Lem Cameron made the first hostile move the night Mort hung him, and they couldn't prove he didn't. Tassie came first. He'd see her, tell her exactly what he'd done and why he'd done it; then ask her why she had betrayed him; then give himself up to Walsh.

"Lotta excitement in town lately."

"That so?"

"Yeah. Girl let two outlaws out'n jail an' a third owlhoot shot 'em down ten miles out'n town."

Mort's glance whipped to the barber's face. The man was busy cutting hair. "I know."

The barber darted a sidelong glance at Mort. "Did you know the sheriff locked the girl up?"

The shock was solid. Mort lifted his glance and it locked with the barber's look at Mort through the mirror on the front wall of the room. "No," he said slowly, "I didn't know that."

"Well — he did. Took her in last night and locked her up. Her old man's a pardner or somethin' in the Big Sink Stage Company." The barber's glance dropped away. "But I reckon you know all that," he said quietly.

"Why would I know it?" Mort's glance was steady and unblinking.

The barber answered casually, still cutting Mort's hair: "You're Morton Ramsey, aren't you?"

"Pretty wide awake, Pardner," Mort said.

"Feller gets so's he remembers faces in this business. Especially when there isn't much excitement around anyway. Knew you when you walked in."

"That so?" Mort didn't sound pleased, nor did he look pleasant. The barber's glance crossed with Mort's look once more, then dropped back to his labours.

"Ramsey, I got a wife and two kids. I wasn't raised to mind other folks' business. You got nothing to worry about from me. Only I recognised you right away and figured I'd pass this on to you. You're bein' hunted like a wolf around Clearwater."

"Maybe," Mort said, "Sheriff Walsh could talk you out of what you know, pardner."

The barber shrugged and didn't look up. There were small beads of perspiration on his forehead. "I reckon not. If he finds out you been in town, it'll have to be from someone else who recognises you — not me. Like I said: I got a family. But you got a warnin' coming. That's why I'm talking.

Only reason. I could've just kept shut up, you know."

Mort didn't speak. Some of the determination to do what he'd decided was best, after all, went out of him. He studied the barber's face. The man probably meant what he said. It was an unwritten law of the land for men to say nothing about others, ever. All he wanted was another hour of freedom. He got down out of the chair and reached for the key to the bathroom absently, accepted the frayed towel and chunk of lye-soap, then stood there looking at the barber.

"A man could walk down to the sheriff's place while another man was taking a bath — couldn't he?"

"Yeah," the barber said without blinking, "he could. But he won't."

Mort stared a second longer, then grinned. "All right, hombre. I'll gamble on you. Damned fool thing to do — but I'll take a chance."

The barber climbed into his own clipping-chair and worried-off a corner from a plug of twist, cheeked it deftly, and smiled at Mort.

"What'd a man gain by turning you in? There's no reward, but there's a whale of a chance you might get out and come back."

The smile broadened, took on a rueful look. "Ramsey, you're safer in that tub of mine than anywhere else I know of in town."

Mort took those last words with him into the bathroom and mulled them while he scrubbed. Once he was interrupted when the barber came over to the door and called out: "I'm still here."

It amused Mort. "I wasn't worrying. Wonder if you'd do me a favour?"

"What?"

"Go down to Merk's and buy me a shirt an' a pair of levis."

"Sure. We're about the same size. I'll be right back with 'em."

He was, too; and stood outside the door while Mort dressed. Was watching the renegade with close interest when Mort came out and swept the room quickly; saw no one else there, and fished out a wad of crumpled paper money and passed it over to the barber.

"That's for helping a feller get a little more freedom. An hour or more anyway." With the last word, it dawned on him. Tassie wouldn't be at home. He frowned. "Won't need that much time, after all."

The barber glanced up from the currency. There was puzzled concern in his glance. "You — aren't givin' up, are you?"

"Yeah. Just thought of something. I'm going to offer Walsh a trade. Me for the girl. Think he'll do it?"

The expressive eyes looked worried. "You're bein' foolish, Ramsey. He wants you for murder. Hell — he'll have to turn her out in a day or so anyway. Can't hold her long just for turnin' those Camerons out. But with you, it's different."

"Yeah," Mort said drily. "I'm a murderer. That's a hell of a lot different. He ought to trade then, I reckon, and be glad to."

The barber shrugged. "It's your business, not mine," he said. "Anythin' I can do for you while you're in Walsh's can?"

"No thanks. *Adios*."

"*Adios,* Ramsey, and — good luck." He said it like a man who wished it when he knew it wasn't a minimum possibility at all.

Mort went out into the heat, felt it lash him across the ribs as he started up the plank-walk towards the sheriff's office. He felt like a man who was out of breath and within sight of shore; wanting to make it the worst way and wondering if he could. So far, this short walk was the most dangerous thing he'd undertaken. The land was full of unknowns with itching trigger-fingers. Men — like Jay had been — who had yet to make their reputations on either side of the law.

Mort Ramsey, wanted killer, was legal game. He belonged to the black brotherhood who could be shot down on sight by anyone, any way it could be done, from front or rear.

And the saturnine little fate that had been dogging him for days now, came out to sneer at him once more, with perfect timing. He wasn't twenty feet from Walsh's office when the single explosive eruption came, bracketting-out the dull noises of everyday living. Only one thing saved the hunted man. Split-second recognition a fraction before the gun went off, that was inspired by his nervous feeling that guns might be trained on his back as he went up-town; seeing recognition on men's faces as he walked.

That keyed-up tension, like a coiled spring, was what kept him alive. The thunder of the shot found him moving sideways ahead of it. At the echo, mingled with the startled, astonished shouts, he was sprinting for the narrow alleyway where Tassie had held a gun on him once.

Sweat stood out on his upper lip and his forehead, oiled his gun-palm and was sticky under his shirt. Crouched and shaken, he felt the reverberation through the thin wall when the door to the sheriff's office slammed open and closed.

"Who did that?"

Mort knew the voice instantly. He'd heard it the last time from behind a mothy old chair at the Cameron ranch. Sheriff Walsh. He pushed back deeper into the cool shadows of the narrow walk-way, waiting. A form shot past, moving fast. Mort eased his gun down. Walsh was heading across the roadway in a fast, angry walk. His bearing was stiff and outraged. Smiling lopsidedly, Mort holstered his gun and eased himself backwards towards the duckboards, took a long, very careful look in the direction of the single rifleshot, saw nothing suspicious and stepped out on to the planks. He was turning, with only a few feet to go, when the gun roared again. That time he didn't move backwards at all.

An overwhelming nausea churned up from the pit of his stomach. He tried to swear but couldn't find the breath; turned, gun out and coming up. A little drift of dirty grey powder was snaking its way from the front window of a neat little house down and across the road. He watched the traffic disintegrate until only a few hastily deserted saddlehorses stood in bewilderment where their riders had left them, then he fired.

The rifle crashed once more. Mort went

down and couldn't help himself. He rolled over and tasted the salt-blood in his mouth, and fought to bring the gun up. It was quivering so badly he croaked a curse at it, hauled back the dog and tugged off the shot. The rifle didn't reply. It was just as well. Mort Ramsey was face-down, half-on, half-off, the plank-walk. Blood dripped slowly, thickly, into the churned dust, and big blue-bottle flies hurried out of nowhere to settle around it.

"He's gone." Someone shouted it, then there was a muffled tirade of frenzied cursing, and Sheriff Walsh was coming back up the middle of the road with his face working in fury and his cocked .45 weaving uncertainly in his fist.

By the time L. C. Walsh got up beside Mort, there were six men standing over him in limp silence, staring down. One nudged the freshly barbered body with a pointed boot toe. "He sure was game, warn't he? I watched him; he tried like the devil to get off his shots."

"Shut up and fetch the sawbones. No — damn you; not at his house, he isn't there. Look down at the morgue shack. He might be plugging-up those Camerons. If he isn't there —" It drifted off as Walsh knelt, holstered his gun with pursed lips, and rolled

Mort over. "Trap was too good," he said aloud, to no one in particular. "She drew him all right, like I figured she would. Like the Camerons did — but someone else knew she was here an' that he'd come back for her. That stinkin', rotten brother o' his. Damn! I wish to hell he'd killed him at Dead Water. That four-flushing little son of —"

"Out of the way, L.C. Do your cussin' somewhere else."

The doctor elbowed the sheriff out of his way and bent almost double, staring. A second later he straightened up with a startled look and jerked a thumb over his shoulder. "Get a couple of men here to carry him down to my place. He's still alive."

Walsh fixed the doctor with a cold eye. "Like hell I will. His brother just ran out of your place."

"He couldn't have. He had a compound —"

"I don't give a damn if he had two heads and both of 'em were busted. He took three shots at Mort, then beat it out the back way, stole your horse and lit out."

The doctor looked stunned, but he didn't hesitate for long. "All right; all right. Take him into your office then, but don't just stand there. He's bleedin' like a stuck hog."

"There isn't any other damned way to bleed," the sheriff growled, glaring down at Mort and motioning indiscriminately to the crowd for hands. "You there — Lewt and Pete — fetch him inside."

Without another glance at the body and its grunting carriers, Sheriff Walsh stamped into his office, stood aside as Mort was lugged in, motioned callously towards a cot in the corner where the night man usually slept, and stared icily at the craning-necked crowd. "What you buzzards want? Pick the bones? Go on back where you came from." Walsh slammed the door, leaned on it and looked over indignantly at Mort and the busy doctor, then crossed the office to the cell-room beyond it. Just inside the door he fished up a big brass key he'd taken to carrying with him since the Camerons had been liberated, and hefted it, staring at the only occupied one of his strap-steel cages.

"Tassie: you hear that shooting?"

The girl's face, wan and strained, looked up apathetically. There was moving misery in the background of her eyes. An apathy that was hurt and disbelief together. She nodded without speaking.

"Well — that was the hombre you've been thinking ran out on you."

"MORT!" She went up against the steel

straps, hard, holding them with both hands. "It can't be. Sheriff, it can't —"

"It was, girl," Walsh said gruffly, having trouble keeping his cold glance on her face. "That no-account brother of his out-guessed me. He was waiting for Mort to come back for you, just like I was. He got him first. I didn't even —"

"Let me out of here! Please — oh, please! Let me see him, Sheriff."

Walsh unlocked the brass padlock with maddening deliberateness, speaking as he did so. "Tassie — you go home now. When I want you I'll come for you. *If* I want you. Way things're going, I'll be darned if I know who I want from one minute to the next. Just stay in town and I'll —"

She burst past him, flinging the door back so that he had to move swiftly or be struck by the thing. He looked after her with a fiery glance. "Woman! Damned women! Man couldn't blow her out of Clearwater now with a ton of black powder. Well — at least she got him to come in, so she served her purpose with me, anyway."

He pocketed the big key and gave the steel door he'd narrowly missed being hit with, a vindictive kick. "Phew! There wasn't much give in the panel!" Stalking back into the office, he glowered at the two staring riders who had carried Mort Ramsey into his office. "Well, you boys lose something in here?" The riders looked up, startled; glanced back at the bared, broad torso of the unconscious wounded man, and shrugged. Walsh crossed the room in dour silence, opened the street door for them and slammed it over their last footsteps, leaned against it again and fished around for a smoke.

Tassie stood rigid, fighting valiantly against the horror and illness within her. The doctor looked up quickly, saw in a flash what was likely to happen, and averted it with the intuitive ability of his profession.

"Tassie: go next door to Manuel's place and fetch me a big pan of boiling water. Fast, girl!"

"Doctor — will he —"

"Get the water!"

She went, moving so rapidly L.C. barely had time to get out of her way as she groped for the door latch. Watching the door with a jaundiced eye, he escaped injury the second time by being aware of Tassie's preoccupation and stepping clear of the panel. Then he kicked it closed behind her and grunted. The doctor turned and looked up at him.

"Well, Sheriff; you've got your man."

"Sure; but for how long?"

The doctor glanced briefly at Mort. "Oh

— he'll make it all right, but don't tell the girl that. I've been wrong before. Might be a complication set in. You can't ever tell."

"Like cholera, for instance?"

"Well, he was with your brother, you know. He's the only one. That's why I've been so insistent that you catch him. Get him isolated. I still don't see how your brother lived through it. It's a miracle. His age — and all alone — and all."

Walsh nodded through the tobacco smoke. "He was about over it by the time Ramsey here, showed up."

The doctor made an impatient gesture. "Makes no difference. Cholera's highly contagious at any stage."

"Ramsey didn't stay long. Tom said so."

"I know that," the doctor said cryptically, "better than you do. The point is, L.C., your brother's the only one in the territory who's had it, so far. Ramsey here is the only one he exposed to it."

"All right," L.C. said acidly, "I've heard all this before. I'll keep him isolated for you — with pleasure."

The doctor was probing again when Tassie came back with a bucket of steaming water. The sheriff took it from her, kicked up a chair and put the bucket on it. For the first time he got a good look at the bullet holes. He sucked on his cigarette, sensing the girl's nearness, and cleared his throat.

"Missed with the first one, I see." No one spoke. "One in the ribs and one through the — well — he must've been turning or standing sideways when he caught that one. Right through the — ham." He turned suddenly on the girl. "You'd best lope for home, girl."

"No," she said softly, "not just yet, Sheriff. Please — maybe there's something I can do."

The doctor twisted his neck, studied Tassie impassively for a second, then glanced at L.C. and jerked his head towards the door. Sheriff Walsh reached down firmly and took hold of Tassie's arm.

"Come on. He'll be all right with us. You don't have to stare holes in him the first day."

She would have held back but the sheriff was a large man. He eased her outside, closed the door in the face of a look he couldn't meet, latched the door from the inside, and turned and swore softly to himself.

"Doc: how about her?"

"Absolutely not!"

"She's going to be damned hard to keep out of here."

The doctor answered without looking round when he rose from beside Mort. "That's your department. Keep her out just like everyone else. Or you can lock her up with him — but remember what I told you. He's got to be kept absolutely isolated until we're absolutely sure he doesn't have it. It's got to be kept a secret from him just like everyone else, too. All we need is for word to leak out and there'll be the darndest stampede in the country you ever saw. I told you last —"

"I know what you told me — damn it," Walsh said testily. "I was just asking, is all. She'll be worse'n a tick until he's out of here."

"Your department, L.C. See you tomorrow morning, bright and early."

"Early," Walsh growled, opening the door for the doctor; watching him duck past the throng of loafers who were outside waiting eagerly for any morsel of information; and closed the door again.

And when Mort regained consciousness late that evening he looked across the office at the slumped, tired-looking lawman — who was regarding him with a baleful, fixed stare — and tried to grin. "Did he get me bad, Sheriff?"

"Depends on what you call bad. No — you'll live. Live to hang, if you're lucky."

"Who did it? You get him?"

"No, I didn't get him! It was your crawlin' little brother — that's who it was."

Mort's stare held in near-disbelief. "Jay . . . ?"

"Yeah; Jay. Wish to the devil you'd killed him outright over at Dead Water."

"But — how'd he get away?"

Walsh slouched forward in his chair, put his face in his hands and looked past Mort at the wall. "He was too bad off to move, Doc said. I think he was acting it for Doc's sake. Anyway, I locked your girl up because I figured you'd come back for her, seein' she was in bad trouble and all. Was gamblin' on it like I gambled on you coming for the Camerons. With the Camerons, you foxed me through Tassie. All right; if you'd of done it again, I'd of been wrong all around. I gave you the chance. You came back all right — she said you wouldn't — only when Jay heard she was in jail he must've done a little figuring on his own. He got Doc's old carbine and lay behind that front window waiting for you. You can guess the rest. Soon's he saw you, he commenced shooting."

"He was bad off, I heard. Shot up pretty badly."

Walsh shrugged. "Like I said, I think now

128

he was faking most of it." Exasperation was in the lawman's voice. "How the devil else did he work it?"

Mort ignored the question. "Why didn't Tassie think I'd come back?"

Walsh began to twist-up another cigarette. "Maybe she was half hoping you wouldn't. She knew I was using her to draw you in, Ramsey. Maybe she was half discouraged, too — or something."

Mort's conscience pricked him. "Maybe she just plain didn't trust me, too."

Walsh smoked dourly; spoke without looking down at Mort. "She said that, too. Maybe she had a shot of that female intuition women're supposed to have."

Mort lay in silence for a moment, looking up at the fly-specked ceiling. "Sheriff! Did she tell you I was still in the country when you ambushed me at the Cameron place?"

"No-o-o-o; not exactly. I heard her talking to her dad one evening. The way she stuck up for you made me think she knew something. I figured from there. You'd seen her lately: I could tell that from things she said. I knew you wanted the Camerons pretty bad; so — what the hell! — the natural thing was to stake you out. I did — and except for that cinch trick you pulled, I'd of gotten you."

Mort listened with relief. "How about Dead Water?"

"You mean, did she steer me out there?"

"Yeah; that's exactly what I mean."

Walsh's icy glance dropped to Mort's face. He wasn't long in speaking. "She told me that, all right; but for your own darned good. Made me promise not to shoot you even if you showed fight."

"That so?" Mort said sardonically. "When I saw your posse, and all those guns showing, it didn't exactly look like you were out on a social call."

"What'd you expect, Ramsey? You're a murderer in the eyes of the law. I went prepared, and told the possemen to do likewise. I had no intention of gunning you if it was at all possible not to; but I'm a lawman, not a preacher: guns're my trade like men like you are my livelihood. If you think I'm going to play Indian with you — you're crazy. I told Tassie I'd give you better'n an even break — beyond that, I'd bring you in dead or alive. That's all there was to it. Just how the devil'd you get away *that* time?"

"Saw you coming in plenty of time to ride out. So she told you where I was." Mort said it dully, still looking up at the dirty ceiling.

Walsh snorted and leaned back in his chair. "Let me tell you something, my

Christian friend, in case you're holding it against her that she tried to make me save your neck in spite of you. Balance that play of hers off against what she did for you when she let those damned Camerons loose. She made it so's you could square away for Pat Reilly. That's something you couldn't have done for yourself. Listen: if ever a girl's worried herself sick to help a man, that girl's been doing it for you. Personally, I don't think you're worth the effort — and besides that, if it hadn't been for her I'd of nailed your hide to the barn long ago."

"Would you?" Mort fired back, glancing over at the sheriff. "For killing Grat and Davis?"

Walsh snorted. "Hell, no. I don't even need your word that they jumped you two to one. The sign was all around 'em. That was self-defence, and good riddance, as far as I'm concerned. What you're in hot water for is Lem Cameron. For lynching him without giving him a chance."

"He gave Pat Reilly a chance, didn't he?"

"I'm not concerned over Pat Reilly, dammit."

"I reckon not, L.C. Pat was an honest man. All you're interested in is the law breakers. The Pat Reillys in the world have to get killed in cold blood before you damned lawmen do anything about it."

Sheriff Walsh, never a patient man, was reddening in the face. "Let a man get beyond the law and I take an interest in him. Until he does, it's none o' my business what he does. Anyway — Pat Reilly was abetting you when he got it."

"That makes it right to string him up, doesn't it?"

"Of course not, but —"

"But, hell!" Mort flared. "I only did what your lousy law might have done, if it didn't turn Pat's lynchers loose for lack of evidence, or something just as silly. Well, I'm not ashamed of it — and besides that, Lem Cameron made the first lunge in our little fight; I didn't."

"But you hung him."

"Yeah; and I'd do it again if I had the chance. If you'd been on their trail after the stage robbery —"

"I don't have a crystal ball!" Walsh roared.

"You ought to get one, then," Mort snarled back. "I hung a man for murder, Sheriff; exactly what your legal hangman does every day. If I'm guilty of murder, he's guiltier 'cause he's done it oftener."

"That's different, Ramsey: now shut up!" Sheriff Walsh was wrestling heroically with his temper. He could see with half a glance that the wounded man was badly upset and excited. If the doctor should happen in he'd raise the roof. Walsh clamped his teeth close over the anger behind them, but it was Mort himself who dampened the lawman's wrath, unknowingly, when next he spoke.

"Why don't you rake up a posse and get after my brother?"

Walsh settled back and exhaled from a fresh cigarette; made a slighting motion with one hand and let his breath out in a long, slow sigh. "Don't have to. Sent my two deputies out with five possemen. They'll have him before sundown — unless I'm mistaken."

Mort put his head back against the old coat someone had thoughtfully provided for his head. It smelled of old human and horse sweat. "You're gambling on Jay's being too weak to ride far. That it?"

"Right. He won't last under this sun. Not in his shape."

"Maybe he's thought ahead to a hideout, Sheriff."

"Yeah; maybe."

"I'm going to tell you something, Sheriff," Mort said abstractedly, looking at nothing in the air above his cot. "The Ramseys're a tough breed. They don't give out."

Walsh inhaled deeply, exhaled and shook his head from side to side matter-of-factly. "They may be tough, but they're flesh and blood. A man doesn't go far with a cracked skull. Not even a tough one."

Mort lapsed into silence and Walsh sucked on his cigarette to pass away the time. Only once more did they speak, and that was when Walsh said, out of a clear sky:

"Obliged to you, Ramsey, for helping my brother out like that."

"I didn't do it for you, Sheriff."

After that the silence grew and thickened, with Walsh's full approval. He was weary through and through, and there was no relief in sight. Not until one or both of his deputies returned — and the Lord knew when that might be. He found consolation in tobacco. Before Mort broke the hours-long silence again there was a growing plethora of cigarette-butts around the sheriff's chair.

"Tassie. She's so darned young to be in a mess like this."

Walsh grunted and spat, cleared his throat and spat again. "You're a little late thinking of that, aren't you?"

"I didn't bring her into it."

"Maybe not, but you're sure as hell the one that's keeping her in it."

" 'Reckon."

"Thanks," Walsh grunted sarcastically.

Mort looked over at him. "When'll she come and see me?"

"She won't."

"What're you talking about? Hour or so ago you said she —"

"That she's in love with you — the fool. Sure — but that doesn't mean you get any visitors."

"Are you telling me I can't see her?"

"Yeah. Her or anyone else."

"What the devil do you think you're —"

"Oh, shut up," Walsh said placidly, with no particular animosity in his voice. "You can't have any visitors for a week — maybe a month, or even longer, for all I know."

"Why not?" Mort's indignation was suddenly giving way to a sense of bewilderment. The sheriff didn't sound like he was restricting his prisoner so much as it sounded like he was quarantining him.

"Just because you can't. Now shut up, will you?"

Mort lay back, staring at the lawman. After a while he made a sound that was rather like a defiant growl, and closed his eyes; only to open them a moment later and look fixedly at the ceiling again. Walsh wasn't paying his prisoner any attention or he would have noticed the intent look on

Mort's face: as though he was absorbed in thought over something that had just occurred to him.

"Where'd your deputies expect to find my brother?"

Walsh shrugged. "Track him if they can. They had no more idea where he'd headed for than I have."

"You tried tracking him before. Jay's no fool: he'll make for rocky country like he did when he lit out for Dead Water after that stage robbery."

"I reckon," Walsh said, yawning. "But he didn't get much of a start on 'em this time."

"If they can get him in sight before sundown they might get him."

"I'm banking on that. Also on the fact that he'll give out before then. Two to one odds, as I see it."

Mort rolled his head tentatively on the smelly pillow. "You're fooling yourself, Sheriff. Ramseys don't give out."

Walsh didn't bother answering. He made up another cigarette and smoked it absently. Speaking more to himself than to his prisoner, he leaned over and craned a look out the tiny window in the front wall of his office. "I wish to hell they'd get back. I'm tired all the way through."

"Go to sleep," Mort said matter-of-factly.

L. C. Walsh — with or without reason — was a suspicious man. He cocked a chary eye at Mort and coughed. "Can you stand up and walk?"

"Don't know; but I'll try. Why?"

The sheriff jerked a thumb towards the strap-steel cages visible beyond the opened door at the back of the room. "You could bed down in there. Then I could sleep, too."

Mort pushed himself part way up, winced with pain and felt the perspiration leap out of his body. The pain was bad enough; making it appear more than it was was no great chore. He held himself up for a second, then went back down, very slowly, with a rueful little tug of his head and a throttled groan.

"I might, Sheriff, if you'd carry me."

"No; forget it. Might start the holes to leakin' if we did that. Doc'd raise the roof."

Mort lay still, eyes closed and breathing unevenly, counting the seconds; gathered them into minutes which he harnessed into an hour; then, eventually, two hours; and beyond that he couldn't force himself to keep up the illusion. Rolling his head gently, he looked at the sheriff. Walsh was asleep, mouth agape, emitting turbulent, deep sounds of bronchial insurrection, slouched-over and dead-looking.

It took half an hour for the wounded man to stand erect. He had to hold tightly to a peg in the wall, for support, and wait until the myriad spirals died out inside his head, before he dared risk a step. The pain in his hip was excruciating; far worse than the sting along his ribs where Jay's slug had spun him with its nearly fatal impact. But he could move, finally, without the giddiness — just the agony of his wounds to plague him.

He made it to the sheriff's cluttered desk, picked up a carelessly thrown-down handgun — which happened to be his own — hefted it, and moved laboriously over towards Sheriff Walsh. One short, arching, solid blow, and the lawman slid fluidly out of his chair into an inartistic heap on the cigarette-butt littered floor. Mort stood above him, breathing in quick, ill gasps, trying to minimise the stabs of flame-like agony along his ribs; waiting. L. C. Walsh didn't move. The sounds of Clearwater's early evening came faintly through the walls of the office to Mort.

It wasn't an easy thing to shrug into the blood-stiff new shirt, scoop up his hat, holster the gun, and cross to the doorway to listen. He did it slowly, painfully — because he had to; drove himself to do it. He lowered the lamp-mantle and blew down upon the flame, crossed to the door again and opened it, let the coolness of descending dusk revive him for a second, then very slowly, awkwardly, he moved down the back alleys towards the edge of town, where his horse was tied. The shadows were long enough: he could have passed for a drunk easily. His wan face with its feverish eyes was shielded beneath the jerked-down hat-brim.

He had to grit his teeth hard and close his eyes with the effort of swinging up into the saddle. His horse, stiff from standing so long, obeyed the reins sluggishly. He turned and rode due south until the lights of Clearwater were like tiny stationary fireflies, then swung west for a while, and finally rode a course that was northerly too.

The night advanced with a coolness to offset his fever. It brought up fancied images, like mirages, to capture his wandering attention. Spun out macabre dramas that were forgotten fragments out of his early life. Brought them up with such vivid closeness that he hardly noticed the passage of time.

Three times he had to stop and rest, and once he had to tighten the slippery bandages the doctor had bound him with. Especially the one the saddle touched. He didn't bleed much; the sullen swellings took care of closing-off the tears in his flesh; but he was light-headed, and only rest seemed to help that. At last he tried to ride standing in his stirrups, right hand clutched around the saddle-horn, but his strength wasn't equal to the effort for more than minutes at a time. To Mort, time was something fixed and unmoving. It was an everlasting substance that was warm and cloying to him. An eternity of dull ache and yawning consciousness that rose and fell, rose and fell, in a monotonous cycle of faintly heard hoofbeats.

Then came the time when he couldn't stand the effort any longer, and dismounted so awkwardly that he ended up his descent in a grotesque tumble; sprawling arms and legs and a face as pale as bloodless flesh could be. Sleep, of a kind deeper than usual, came quickly and benevolently. His horse moved off a little way, glanced back several times, then lowered his head to graze.

Out of the shadow world of faint greys Mort emerged, hours later, more dead than alive — but with a vivid picture of Jay in his mind. He lay still, appalled at the clarity of the vision and only slightly revived from the rest. He licked his lips and swore aloud. Of course! Why hadn't he thought of it before?

Sheriff Walsh was right. No matter how tough a breed a man was, no one could travel far with a badly injured body. Who would know better? He was no better off than Jay; maybe even not as well off.

Jay would have thought ahead on that. He'd been lying in his comfortable ambush for a long time. He would have worked out all the details long before he threw down on Mort. He'd have it all fixed in his mind where he was going after he killed Mort. It wouldn't be far off, either, and it would be some place he knew, and where the law would have trouble finding him — tracking him.

Mort felt his strength coming back a little at a time, like water seeping into a bucket with a crack in it. He made no move to rise, beyond looking around for his horse; and when he did the vision of his brother was very clear.

Jay couldn't go to Tassie for sanctuary, even if he knew she wasn't in jail any more. He dared not stay in Clearwater. There were only two shale rock-patches in the Paiute Valley where he could lose a posse. One was out at Dead Water, and Jay couldn't begin to ride that far before he fell off his horse and passed out. Besides, Walsh would send men out there first thing. It would have to be the other rock slick, then. The one that ran, like a shiny granite belt, right smack between Mort's ranch and the Pat Reilly place, almost east and west for over three miles. If Jay had ridden over that rock slick and into Pat's range beyond where Pat's and Mort's horses would be — there wouldn't be any way to tell one track from another, even if the law tracked him that far — which wasn't likely. No lawman would expect to find Jay Ramsey hiding near the house of the man he had caused to by lynched.

Mort got up and started weakly for the horse. Jay was more deadly wounded than unhurt. Pat's widow was alone. Jay was like a blind rattler now. He caught the animal easily and felt stronger when he mounted; winced with an indrawn breath from contact with the saddle, and nudged the animal out.

He rode with his teeth clenched, for the pain was worse, even though his strength seemed to have returned in sufficient quantity to enable him to sit the saddle easily. Sweat glistened on his face, went ignored in the face of what lay ahead, and the late night's benign brush on his face was pleasant. He rode slowly, watching the dim, murky trail ahead and checking his deductions over and over again. If he was right, Jay wouldn't be many miles away. If he was wrong, he lacked the strength to make a sustained flight and would have to give himself up again.

There was surcease from his constant doubts when he warily approached his own place, spent a long hour reconnoitering the yard and buildings — only to conclude that, if Jay had been there, he had gone on. Riding just as slowly as before, Mort headed for the Reilly ranch. The stars winked wickedly down at him, and the Comanche moon shed an unreal light, opaque and dull, over the world he rode through. His light-headedness had vanished, but the dead, silent land he traversed aided in creating a similar illusion of unreality.

Once in the near distance he saw several horses chasing another animal that appeared to be in headlong flight towards Clearwater. It was a suspicious and ominous thing to a born-and-bred horseman. The fleeing horse would be a stranger to the other animals. They would resent him as an intruder. There was an excellent chance that the fleeing horse might be the one Jay had stolen when he'd fled from town. Mort reached down the side of his saddle and tugged his carbine loose, brought it up out of the saddle-boot twice, to make sure it was riding free, then let it drop back. He might not get more than one or two quick shots. If Jay was up ahead at the weathered buildings of Pat Reilly's place, he would be watching if he was able to do so. Mort meant to take no chances.

He swung his mount in a big circle and came into the Reillys' yard from the rear of the barn, keeping the dark outline of the building between himself and the house. Riding slowly, his horse's tread muffled in the thick dust, Mort stopped often to study the place. Nothing was moving — but then, the hour was late. Satisfied at long last that the barn, at least, was safe to approach, he reined up and swung down. Stood motionless on the far side of his horse, feeling the night, peering intently for sign of movement, and listening, too. There wasn't even lantern light in the house, dimly silhouetted against the night sky.

Mort brought his horse up into the barn, using the beast as a shield; found the barn deserted; slipped open a stall door and put the animal inside — but didn't remove the bridle or even loosen the cinch. If anything went wrong he'd need his horse in a hurry, more than likely.

There was an eeriness to the Reilly place

that Mort could feel in large measure. He squinted at the front opening of the barn and saw the spot where he and Pat had squatted with the stone crock of whisky between them, the day he'd come back from the fatal meeting with Jay at Dead Water. He'd been sick with the thought that he had killed his own brother, that day. Now, he hoped fervently that Jay was close by. He wanted to kill him. He had never had many illusions about his brother; only a few vague hopes that Jay might straighten out sometime. Those hopes were as dead as they could be, now. Only a rope or a bullet would jerk the slack out of Jay Ramsey. Mort had both; one in his hand as he stole through the old barn, the other hanging coiled on the swells of the saddle. He wanted a chance to use one or the other — and soon.

A kicked-up flake of hay caught his attention halfway through the barn. He stopped, turned and stared at it. Grunted softly, went over and pushed the loose chaff aside with a boot-toe. There was no sense of surprise in him at what he saw; just a grim feeling of triumph. A saddle, blanket and bridle, lying under the hastily contrived concealment. Thrown down in careless haste and covered over with loose hay. Mort reached down and touched the blanket. It was clammy-wet and cool. His brother had been on the ranch for at least two hours; maybe longer. Protected like that, a sweaty saddle-blanket would take a long time to dry stiff.

Pat Reilly had always been a man who refused to clutter-up his yard with the usual haphazard out-growth of little buildings. Tack-house, grainery, chicken-house and the like. Mort raised his glance from Jay's tack and swept the night beyond with a cold glance, and was thankful for Pat's orderliness. Aside from the main house, there was nothing to obstruct his view — or conceal his brother — between the barn's front opening and the house, which was distant enough to be little more than a bulky, harsh blob of blackness with squared corners against a slightly lighter skyline.

There was a little spring-house off to one side of the main house, but beyond that necessary adjunct to rural living there was nothing to interfere with Mort's view. Jay would likely be in the house all right, but the spring-house was a possibility, too. Mort hefted his gun and stared into the night. Unless Jay was keeping a close watch, Mort might be able to cross the barren yard with safety. If he was watching — which was more than just possible, since he was a hunted man — Mort wouldn't get ten feet into the clearing before he'd be shot down.

He studied the outline of the house and listened for night sounds. The building was dark and forbidding-looking, and the little creatures of the dark hours were silent, adding to the sense of impending disaster that permeated the darkness and made Mort's flesh crawl, in spite of himself. He licked dry, cracked lips and tried to think of a way to cross the open ground to the house.

A long way off a coyote sounded. It was a haunting, macabre noise, that added to the brooding loneliness he felt. With an effort he shook off his black mood, shifted his footing and swore, then squatted and skylined the house. There was no movement at all; nothing visible that shouldn't have been — and yet he knew Jay was close by. Wondering if Carrie Reilly was on the place — and, if so, if his brother had harmed her — he rose, winced from the angry reminder his body offered that his wounds were still open, and walked out beyond the barn's front doorway. There he stopped, picked up a stone, held it thoughtfully for a second, then dropped it with another oath. Jay wouldn't be fooled that way and Mort would give himself away by throwing the thing. He hunkered, leaned back against the barn, and considered ways of getting close enough to the house to find his brother. Each idea that came up was faulty. He discarded them one by one. The idea that eventually appealed to him brought him up again and sent him stalking back into the barn.

Unsaddling his horse didn't take long. It was like burning his bridges behind him, in a way; but Jay was also afoot now. In his concentration on Jay, it never occurred to him that his brother might not be his only enemy in the night. He was too engrossed in the work at hand to spend time in reflection. Leading his horse by the mane, Mort took the animal out of the barn and led him in an ambling, careless-appearing walk across the yard. He even stopped and let the animal snuffle the dust now and then, giving the illusion that the beast was a stray, loose in the house area.

It was perilous work at best, but Mort kept the animal between his body and the house and trusted to the darkness to conceal his legs when he missed keeping in step with the horse.

He got close enough finally to risk a glance at the geranium bed Pat's wife had carefully cultivated with the rinsings from the water bucket. He was gauging the distance, and wondering if he dared run for it, when Jay's voice — recognisable, cold and knife-edged — ground out harshly at the horse.

"You! Get out of there! Huh — git!"

The horse threw up his head in sudden astonishment. Mort lost his hold on the mane. The animal sensed its freedom and shied away with a soft snort when Jay unleashed a string of scorching oaths at it. For a fleeting second Mort was exposed, then he moved with desperate speed and threw himself into the tangle of flowers and weeds, panting and crawling with apprehension. The moment he lay there fumbling to bring his six-gun to bear seemed an eternity, but the suspense didn't last long, at that. Jay's violent profanity ripped the darkness with its frenzied, abrupt fury and consternation. He had seen someone — a man — for a second, and realised the horse had been a blind after all.

Mort pressed in against the house. He was holding his breath when the shattering, deafening roar of a carbine exploded from within the house. Dirt and dust flew a yard south of him. He could smell crushed vegetation and gunsmoke when he raised his hand-gun and fired at the orange-yellow tongue of carbine flame. Tinkling glass and a howl of wrath answered the pistol shot.

Then Mort crawled fast. Was still crawling when Jay pin-pointed him with two fast shots, one on either side of where he'd been; then a slower, more deliberate third shot, squarely in between the first two. Mort winced as much from the understanding of how dead he would have been if he hadn't moved, as he did from the angry protest from his wounds.

"Walsh? You'll never take me alive, damn your soul. I've got Carrie Reilly in here. She'll go before I do."

Mort edged closer to the baseboard of the house before he risked an answer. "This isn't Walsh, Jay. This is Mort. If you touch —"

"Mort!" The voice was solid with stunned disbelief. "I don't believe you."

"Come out and take a look. You're not much of a rifle shot, Jay, if you thought you downed me for good in front of Walsh's place."

There was a long moment of silence while the forted-up outlaw digested the astonishment and recognised the voice of the man he was sure he had killed; then, quite suddenly, his thin laugh broke into the quiet.

"You're not so good yourself, Mort. Thought you'd downed me for good out at Dead Water, didn't you?"

"Yeah. Wish I had, Jay. Come out of there unarmed."

Another rattling, mirthless laugh. "Sure; and you'll promise me a fair trial."

"I promise you nothing, but if you don't come out of there I'll come in and get you. What've you done to Pat's wife?"

"She's tied to a chair in here. She's my ace in the hole. Mort? Get yourself a horse and ride out of here."

"When I go, you'll go with me."

"Like hell! If you don't get out of here I'll kill you, that's my word on't."

"Come on out and try it," Mort taunted. He could hear his brother swearing in a steady monotone. He knew Jay would have to expose himself in order to fire down the side of the house at him. His eyes burned from watching the shattered window where Jay had been, not daring to blink; not daring even to whip a glance anywhere else for even an instant. It was an impasse, with Jay Ramsey holding the best hand. At least he wasn't exposed — and Mort was. If the siege lasted until dawn, Mort's chances of survival would be materially lessened. Time would play into Jay's hands. Mort's dilemma was increasing in his mind when Jay called out again. The nervousness in his brother's voice reassured him a little, but didn't alter things much.

"Mort — damn your coyote heart — this is your last chance to walk down to the barn, saddle up, and get t'hell out of here."

Mort ignored the ultimatum. "Let Carrie come outside, Jay, then maybe we can talk."

"The devil!" Jay shot back. "I wouldn't trust you any farther'n I could throw you. Not after what you did at Dead Water."

Mort's anger flashed anew. "Jay — you're crazy. I tried every way under the sun to talk you out of fighting me at Dead Water, and you know it. Before you killed Dell Forrest, all the law wanted you for was robbery. Now it's murder. You had your chance out there, and I'm the one that offered it to you."

"I won't hang any higher for three killings than for one. You're going to be the next hombre I leave face-down — then comes the Reilly woman. How do you like that — bushwhacker?"

Mort edged backwards as he talked, shouting louder than was necessary, to conceal any noise he might make. Working his way towards the corner of the house with painful writhings. "You won't get me, Jay; and if you touch Carrie Reilly I'll run you down like a spinner-wolf, and gut-shoot you to boot. You're a damned fool; why'd you do this to Tassie?"

"Tassie," Jay said suddenly, as though abruptly remembering something long out of mind. "What about her? What've you told her? — damn your eyes!"

Nothing. I didn't have to tell her what you are, Jay — she already knows. In fact, she was the one who told me what you were."

"Liar!" Jay called out. "I heard about you two when I was supposed to be dyin' in the Doc's place. She's in love with you, isn't she? You talked her into lettin' Grat and Dave out so's you could run 'em down. All right; you turned her against me an' you killed the Camerons — but you won't get me like that. How do you like the way I used her, too, when I shot you, Mort?"

There was a ringing taunt in Jay's voice, but Mort ignored it. He was covered with cold sweat by the time he made it around the corner of the house and risked getting to his knees. He glanced back along the side of the house just as Jay's carbine's snout whipped out through the broken window. Mort fired by instinct. It was a near-hit, with the slug smashing into the log siding of the house and grooving-out a wicked dagger-sharp splinter. The carbine jerked back convulsively, then exploded harmlessly. Mort snapped off a second shot as Jay pulled his gun back inside, and howled curses at his brother.

The night sounds were as quiet as death around the yard. Mort got to his feet with an effort, blinked away the shooting pains and leaned against the wall, reloading his gun. At least he could move again, and there was a feeling of security in that, that he'd lacked back there in the geranium bed. He held his hand-gun ready and moved off toward the rear of the house; but his hope to flank his brother was abruptly shattered when he stumbled over a crockery commode bowl on the back porch and smashed it into a dozen pieces. The racket died out swiftly and Mort heard footsteps from inside, moving swiftly towards him. He retreated around the house again, flattened, and waited. There was no shot. The barrier of eerie silence closed in again, heavy with suspense. Danger and death were all around dead Pat Reilly's house.

Mort perspired freely, hardly conscious of his clotted wounds any longer. Unaware what a frightful apparition he made with his blood-stiff shirt and pants, his matted hair, unshaven, sunken-eyed, sallow look, with the lust to kill stamped into the set lines around his eyes and mouth. He stood there, wondering if, after all, the doctor's prognosis had been correct about Jay's skull being fractured. It didn't seem likely; not with Jay using a carbine like that.

Knowing his brother as he did, Mort suspected that Jay's deceit hadn't been altogether confined to duping the doctor either. He shook off the beads of sweat on his forehead. Sheriff Walsh had been fooled, too; otherwise he'd have locked Jay up. Mort made a wry face. Two fools — and he had to undo what had been overlooked by them. He shoved off the wall and moved towards the front of the house again.

The silence rasped nerve-ends raw for both of them, but Mort Ramsey had a different disposition than his brother had. He wasn't living with haunted memories and warped hatreds, either; so it was Jay whose control broke first.

"Mort? Where the hell are you? Listen — I'll make a trade with you."

Mort placed the sound near the door, that was obviously barred from within. He didn't reply, guessing correctly that Jay's bluster wasn't matched by his courage.

"Mort? Damn you — answer me!"

"What kind of a trade?"

"That's better. Listen — you let me walk out of here and ride away and I'll leave Carrie Reilly alone."

"And if I don't agree?"

Jay's voice had a shrill raggedness to it. It made Mort's flesh crawl. "I'll kill her, damn you. I'll shoot her an' toss the carcass out where you can see it!"

Mort understood how close his brother was to cracking. He sucked some cool night air into his lungs and held the silence, thinking. He'd had an uneasy thought at Dead Water, when he'd faced his brother before. Jay wasn't altogether rational at times. Seemed like he was almost insane when the pressure bore down on him. Went berserk, sort of. Now, Mort felt that he would do exactly what he said. He cleared his throat, spat, and called out:

"All right. But I want to see Carrie Reilly walk out of that house before you do, Jay."

"I ain't hurt her," Jay called back quickly.

"Maybe not, but I want to see her myself, first. I want to know she's all right."

"If she is, you won't try to bushwhack me, Mort?"

"No. You can catch your horse and ride."

"Where are you now, Mort?"

"Never mind that. Just cut Carrie loose and let me see her walk out of there. After that, you come out too. Holster your gun, Jay, and don't make any mistakes."

"I'm trusting you," Jay said.

Mort made a face, shook his head and answered: "Then cut Carrie loose."

Mort waited; gun palmed, cocked, and belt-buckle high. The night got as quiet as a tomb again. It had a shaft of chilliness in it, as though dawn wasn't far off. Mort looked over at the eastern horizon, saw no lightness and swivelled his head back in time to see the unmistakable, matronly figure of Pat Reilly's widow stumble out into the yard.

"Carrie? Are you all right?"

"I — guess so, Mort. Stiff, is all. He's coming, Mort. Jay's coming out."

Mort knelt swiftly on one knee and levelled his .45. Jay came haltingly, his head held forward; six-gun holstered but the carbine riding easily on both fists. Mort knew without seeing it that the hammer was back and Jay had a finger curled around the trigger. His mouth pulled down in a bitter smile.

"Mort? You see me? Remember: you gave your word."

Mort's contempt grew. "You're safe enough until you're out of the yard, Jay. Hurry up — move out and don't look back."

Jay hurried, stalked past Carrie Reilly, then abruptly broke and sprinted for the barn. Too late, Mort remembered that his horse was the only one near the barn. He was getting to his feet when he heard Jay's muffled cry of exultation, and knew his horse had been found and caught. Standing there irresolutely, listening to the frantic sounds from the barn, Mort didn't see Carrie Reilly until she was close to him, then he turned sluggishly and faced her.

"Mort — you'll need a horse. He's taken yours."

"They're all turned out, Carrie. I rode through 'em on the way here."

"No. I've kept Pat's stud-horse staked out behind the house. He's up there now. I'll get him."

Mort searched the greying woman's face. "He didn't do anything to you, did he?"

She shook her head. "Just scared me half to death, that's all. Mort, he won't ride far. He's badly hurt. He's got a bandage on his head as big's a mop."

"Yeah," Mort said, not believing. "I'll fetch my gear to the front of the barn if you'll get the stud-horse, Carrie."

Carrie Reilly moved off into the greying darkness. Mort cocked his head, listening. Seconds later he heard his brother riding away. He gauged the speed and direction carefully, then limped down to the barn, dragged his tack painfully outside, and watched Carrie bring the sleek black stallion up. He saddled and bridled the animal, trying hard to conceal from Pat's widow how weak and tired he was, swung into the saddle and forced up a wan smile.

"Thanks, Carrie — about Pat — I don't know what to say."

"Say nothing, Mort. We both feel the same. I — knew my Pat, Mort. He had a way to him. Maybe he could've talked his way out of it; Pat wasn't that kind. I've got a sister in Clearwater. I'm going in to live with her. Mort? Go hunting, son — good luck."

CHAPTER FIVE

How Men Die

Mort felt the tremendous power and brute force under him when he reined the black stud-horse around and lifted him into an easy, gentle lope that buried him in the darkness within four strides. The Reilly place dropped back and became a part of the haunted night that he no longer regarded.

Feeling better, evidently livening-up the reserve of energy within his tough body, Mort looked down at the thick neck of his horse and smiled. He was far better mounted than Jay was. It probably wouldn't be much of a chase, after all — maybe.

And it probably wouldn't have been, either; except that Mort and Jay Ramsey weren't the only horsemen abroad in the purple gloom. Mort was pushing the big horse hard, straining for the sound of a horse in the darkness ahead of him, when he heard instead the ominous rumble of many horses coming. He reined-up in abrupt, startled astonishment, and listened. There were at least five animals making the noise he heard — and possibly twice that number. They were coming fast, and from the direction of Clearwater.

He sat in silence until he heard a man shout, then he eased the powerful stud-horse out into a long-legged lope again and raced away in the direction his brother had taken — only now he was fleeing from a posse he guessed was after both the Ramsey brothers. No sooner had he broken over into to a lope again than the sound of several excited yells split the night. The posse evidently had heard him and was riding after the sound of his hoofbeats. Frantically, Mort considered ways of escaping them as he rode, twisted backwards in the saddle — giving his ham wound a chance to avoid most of the jolting — and at the same time looking into the murky, very limited field of visibility behind him.

He could distinguish the sounds and locations of the possemen, but he couldn't see any of them. It made for a tense situation, for Mort never knew when one of the hard-riding lawmen would see him; but it also gave him time to test the powerful stallion's speed and stamina by keeping out of sight of his pursuers.

The race continued in the ghostly darkness, with Jay fleeing for his life from his own brother, and Mort riding after him on a superior animal, and with a Clearwater posse behind Mort. He was caught between two fires and knew it. Only one source offered any consolation at all: the powerful stallion he rode, fresh and mighty, surging ahead in giant strides that no ordinary horse could equal.

The pursuit went on for a long, fraught hour, then Mort reined-up quickly and listened. The possemen were strung out behind him. Up ahead there wasn't a sound — or if there was, he couldn't distinguish it from the running horses behind him. Astride again but going slower in a sensible effort to conserve his mount, Mort tried to think ahead to where Jay would go. There were many places that were likely, but, following in his mind's eye the route Jay was riding, two places stood out as the most probable destinations of his brother. One was Dead Water again, where Jay had fought his way to freedom once before, with the aid of a miracle, and where he could best hide his tracks; or the deserted, off-trail Cameron ranch, which was on the way to Dead Water. The Cameron place would be on his way, Mort decided, with only a slight detour in the general direction of Dead

Water. He would ride to the Camerons; then, if Jay wasn't there, he'd go directly for Dead Water.

There was the possibility, too, that Jay wouldn't even try to make Dead Water. It was a long way off. Mort nudged the big horse and wagged his head at the possibility. Still, Jay hadn't looked to be on his last legs back at Pat Reilly's place. He might be able to ride that far, at that.

Mort swore aloud, gigged the stallion and headed overland for the Cameron place. He was hoping that the dawn — faintly visible on the horizon, where a knife-slash of pale pink was cutting diagonally across the soft, heavy underbelly of the night — wouldn't betray him to the pursuit. He glanced back often but saw no one, although the sound of horsemen was still behind him. Not as many as there had been, from the sounds, but still there nevertheless.

He rode with his head bent, eyes trying to pierce the gloom for fresh horse tracks. Riding with the smooth ripple of powerful muscle under him, propelling him tirelessly towards the Cameron ranch.

Then the dawn broke over, like an explosion, from the east. Dazzling, brilliant, breathtaking and glaring. It flung light down over the cool rangeland with a profligate generosity that deceived no one. Heat, like hot lead, would follow in an hour or so. Mort used the new daylight to hunt out the possemen. Only four were in sight, riding wearily and determinedly on faltering horses, far behind him. He swung forward and began to zig-zag as he rode, searching intently for fresh horse sign. There was none. Puzzled, he slowed the stallion to a slow trot and bent far over, searching the flinty ground for any kind of an impression that looked fresh at all.

He had to allow the pursuit to get perilously close before he found anything at all, then he let out a long, wavering sigh. Jay was riding for Dead Water, after all; and he was riding over the hardest ground he could find, as well. It jibed with what Mort knew of his renegade brother. Jay was a killer and worse, but he was no fool. The sparse, meagre tracks left by his brother's horse were confined to rock-hard adobe with an uncanny instinctiveness that made Mort marvel how Jay could know the ground so well in the darkness.

Still, Jay was wily. Now, he was desperate as well. There would be only a slight delay in passing through the Cameron place. He swerved the stallion, lifted him into a run with his hooks, and settled their course on a thin spit of trees that edged down out of the uplands and invaded the rangeland a few mile's ahead.

Someone wasted a long carbine shot. Mort twisted and looked back. There were seven riders in view, but only three were close enough to even expect a slug to carry that far. He turned back forward with a sardonic little grin. Wasted lead, that shot.

The sun struck the ground with a flat hand, then balled itself into a monstrous fist and bounced back from a fierce blow to pummel the earth, and everything on it, with the increasing heat. Mort felt the itch of dry, clotted blood along his ribs and fingered gingerly around the bullet crease, scratched it slightly, and watched the trees come up closer as he rocketed towards them. Once in among them, he had instant relief from the sunblast, and reined-up, studying the pursuit again.

The same three riders were still coming on. Evidently the balance of the posse had given up. At least, they weren't in sight. It made Mort think back to the day when he and Dell Forrest had been just as determined in running down the outlaw who later turned out to be Mort's own brother.

Keeping to the trees and riding slowly, letting the stud-horse have a "blow," Mort eased over towards the open land beyond, where the Cameron ranch buildings were. He had lost track of time, and thirst began to bother him about the time the sun was climbing above him. Daring to seek water, he let the stallion scent-up a seepage spring, and both of them drank from scooped-out potholes, then rested a precious moment — Mort staying astride, afraid to get down again after he'd dismounted to drink for fear he would lack the strength to pull himself up the second time. He nudged out the big horse finally, and they went through a thick, fragrant pine-forest with its muffling, spongy undercoating of long, brown pine needles.

When the trees thinned out Mort could see the blistered, writhing, shimmering tumble of the Cameron's corrals and out-buildings. He made the long dash across the open land with a recklessness that was fool-hardy, and only the fact that Jay wasn't lying in ambush, waiting, permitted him to sweep into the yard, pause long enough for a quick look around, then thunder on his way again. There hadn't been a fresh horse-track any-where around the Cameron buildings. More than that, Mort was satisfied his brother wasn't hiding there because his abrupt, rash charge hadn't been met with a fusillade of gunshots — which it certainly would have merited had vindictive, wild-eyed Jay Ramsey seen Mort coming.

Back among the trees again, Mort listened for the possemen but heard nothing. He lined out in a direct route for Dead Water. Left the benign forest finally and was dedicated to his vigil over a scanty trail that writhed under the full blast of the noonday sun. The inferno he rode through was a desert of sand, sage, spiny brush, boulders and desolation. A shunned corner of Nevada where even lizards and rattlers rarely tarried. A lost world of a thousand secrets and tragedies, sifted over with wind-blown sand, pitted boulders and the terrible, merciless heat, and a brooding, evil silence that was laced through with a forbiddingness that was nearly tangible. Mort didn't perspire — he sweated. The water ran off his body in miserly rivulets that were sucked dry almost before they wet his shirt. Ahead, the country shimmered in the throes of cauldron-like, tortured humidity. The faintest stir in the air was a blessing rarely bestowed and beggarly accepted. He hesitated once, briefly, wondering if he shouldn't turn back to the wonderful coolness of the forest, wait for Walsh's posse, and let them take over. No

— this was a personal vendetta.

He rode on, but lowered his head against the fierce whiplash of heat that struck him fully in the face. Far ahead was the beginnings of the rock jumble, and beyond that was Dead Water. And somewhere ahead was Jay, unless he had eluded his brother some way, which wasn't likely with the possemen strung out all over the backtrail. No; Jay would be up ahead all right. Either in the rocky, boulder-strewn prairie itself, or — far more likely — at the closer, more easily defended monolith park around the bad-smelling spring itself.

Drifting along through the leaching heat, Mort remembered how he had felt in the barber's shop. He hadn't cared. There had been a fatal sense of peacefulness, too, that went with the resignation of hope and effort. He looked up and smiled, watching the boulders dance in the heat haze. There was something akin to that other sense of peacefulness within him. He recognised it. It was getting close to the end of the trail. With or without Jay, it was getting close to the end of the trail for Morton Ramsey. He laughed out loud, softly. The stallion's ears shot backwards in surprise. Mort dug out a tobacco sack he'd forgotten he had, created a lumpy cigarette, lit it and exhaled.

"All right, old horse. We've come a long way. Won't be much longer now, I reckon. Either Jay's up there in those damned rocks — or he isn't. If he isn't — then we'll turn right around and head back. Ride right smack-dab into the arms of old Walsh and his posse boys. We'll have done just about all one man and one horse can do, old-timer. After that you'll want some feed, some water and some shade — and I'll want about a month's rest before they string me up. I'll want to sleep for four or five days without even getting up for a drink of water."

Mort's answer to his doubts came so suddenly it jerked him out of the near-delirium he was sinking into, with a violent start. The stallion raised his head and whinnied loudly. If he'd spoken English it wouldn't have been any more eloquent as far as Mort was concerned. Mort thought back to what L. C. Walsh had told him about using a stud horse when he was stalking a man. It made the scarecrow rider smile, in spite of himself. There was a horse or mare up ahead in the rocks. It would be a horse, Mort knew. And — that meant Jay was at Dead Water. How come? Mort wondered. Maybe he'd meant to go farther and couldn't. Whatever had happened, Jay was up there at the scene of his former bloody victory over the law. Up where he'd killed Dell Forrest. Mort slowed a little, certain in his knowledge that the stud-horse had smelled another animal; had nickered to it after the fashion of all stud-horses. He sat for a moment in thought, then tugged out his carbine and stepped down. No sense in risking Pat Reilly's favourite horse. The world was a misty place that shimmered before his eyes. Even so, he exulted inwardly. He'd get one more chance at Jay before Walsh came up — if, indeed, the sheriff was still on his trail.

"Jay!"

Only the solitary echo bouncing off rocks came back. Mort stooped, cradling the carbine. He hobbled the stallion and stood up to wave the animal off, out of carbine range. The animal tossed his head and crow-hopped away from the man.

"Jay — dammit: listen to me!"

"Bang!"

Mort heard the ricochet bullet sing out harmlessly overhead, shook off the annoying sweat and squatted behind a boulder that exuded heat like an oven.

"You damned idiot, Jay! Toss out that gun and walk out of there. Listen — Walsh is behind me. He's after both of us. Come out and give up. You don't stand a chance."

"Neither do you, damn you." The voice was a croak that showed how long Jay Ramsey had been travelling on stamina alone. "He'll gut-shoot you, too, Mort. I hope I can see that when he comes up. I'd give anything I own in this lousy world to see him gut-shoot you, you treacherous, double-crossing —"

"Cut it out, Jay. Get ahold of yourself and listen to me."

"Bang! Bang!"

Mort's anger flared. He threw up his carbine and levered off a shot that sang through the rocks like a bumble-bee, lowered the gun and listened, shouldered it once more and aimed carefully at the big tumble of rocks he thought was shielding his brother, and fired. The dull *thwack!* of the slug carried out over the dead world in echoes that chased one another into oblivion.

"Jay — you haven't got long to make up your mind. They'll be here directly. Come out unarmed and I'll see if Walsh won't give you a fair shake."

Jay laughed. It was an unnatural collection of off-key notes that rose to a crescendo and died away in something that might have been a sob. "You're between two fires, Mort. Damn your lousy soul; you're between me an' Walsh. You're worse off than I

171

am. It's you — brother — that better use your head. Come around these rocks and get in here where I am. Two of us might hold 'em off till dark." Jay laughed again the same way. "Then one of us could ride away. Me, Mort."

Mort flagged a limp sleeve across his face, mopping off the oily sweat. "You're sunstruck, Jay. Sun-crazy. If you buck that posse you'll wind up dead. If you come out and stand trial, you might get off with prison. Listen to me — I'm doing everything I can to save your hide — and you sure don't deserve it from me; but I don't think you know what you're doing. The sun's made you crazy, Jay. Come on out of there."

"Crazy, hell! I'm saner'n you or that posse you're hollering about. I'm crazy like a coyote is. You'll find it out, too, when Walsh's boys ride up an' throw down on you." Jay's laughter erupted and died out as suddenly as it had commenced. "Mort? I'm going to blow your backbone out past your belt buckle. Think *that* over. You always thought you were smart, Mort. Law-abiding and upstanding — and smart. Well — you're a wanted murderer just like I am. The same as me, damn you. Only you're going to hell two jumps ahead of me. That's how smart you turned out to be. Fight your own kin, will you? If I don't send you to blazes first, I hope I'm still able to see you when you get cut down. I'll learn you, you dirty — !"

"Jay," Mort said, almost too quietly for his voice to be heard. "You're not using your head. . . ." He stopped right there. A sudden awareness filled his mind. Actually, his brother wasn't rational. It was more than a term of expression. Jay wasn't right in the head! Maybe it was the sun, after all. Another thought jolted him. That shot of Mort's; the one that had come within a fraction of an inch of killing his brother — it might have deranged him. Mort licked his lips and stirred uncomfortably where he sat.

"Jay? When I shot you out here before, did . . . ?"

"Haw! That shot of yours took off half my ear and ploughed a furrow alongside my head. That's all, Mort. Knocked me out for a few hours. Hell — a lousy shot like you couldn't down me, Mort. Not in a hundred years."

Mort saw a parched straggle of shade and crawled into it; sat back with his carbine over his knees and stared at the natural fortress that protected his brother. Once, he'd been thankful he hadn't killed his brother. Later, he wished he had; even wanted to.

Now, he knew something that even the doctor back in Clearwater hadn't guessed — probably hadn't had a chance to diagnose. Mort's bullet hadn't killed Jay; probably hadn't even fractured his skull — or if it had, not as badly as Jay had led the medical man to think was the case. But — it had done something else. Something appalling and grisly. Something none of them had suspected until that moment. It had, in some ironic, grim way, scrambled his brains. Maybe the concussion had done it; maybe the shock to his nervous system. Maybe anything — but something had done it, all right; for Jay wasn't rational any more. He had always been flighty, unpredictable, savage and ill-tempered; but he had never been irrational before.

Mort sat there thinking about it. Half sick from his own wounds and depressed almost into apathy by the terrible heat. Thinking of how fate had done that to Jay: made him worse than any cougar-bitch at whelping time; more deadly than any blind rattler shedding his skin. And certain, more than ever, that only one thing could stop Jay's madness now. A bullet. One of his bullets, maybe, like Carrie Reilly wanted it to be when Jay went down for the last time.

"Mort? Where are you? Hidin' won't save

you. Where's that posse you said was behind you? Lyin' to me, weren't you? Well — I'm coming after you, big brother: posse or no posse. Goin' to gun you down like I did that other hombre you were out here with before. Dead Water's my lucky spot. You'll see. I'm comin' for you, Mort."

Mort fought off the thraldom. The instinct to survive wasn't as strong as it might have been, but it was there. For no special reason he thought of Tassie Clement. It was another knife-blade turning in his heart. He shrugged it off, leaned forward and cocked the carbine, waiting.

But Jay didn't come. Instead he laughed again. "Thought you'd get another crack at me, didn't you? Guess again, Mort, you damned bushwhacker. I'm no fool. You'll find that out."

Mort silently agreed with Jay. Neither of them was a fool, exactly — but right then Jay was the craftier of the two. Mort was stony-faced from seeing his brother's naked soul revealed before him. Wooden-faced and holding back a hopelessness that was bearing down on him. Jay was out of his mind. Whether it was a temporary or a permanent condition, he didn't know. Might possibly never know. But just the same it made Mort shrink away from the thought of fighting his brother. Shooting a man who wasn't in possession of his faculties had no appeal whatsoever. Mort's hunger for vengeance dimmed; became ashes in his mind.

"Mort? Why don't you say something? Think I don't know where you are? Try this!"

The bullet slammed into flinty rock six feet from Mort's corner of shade, over where he had been and was no longer. The impact scaled off a layer of stone. Laid bare the lighter-coloured rock underneath. Mort stared at it.

"Jay — you damned fool — you're ten yards wide."

"Am I?"

The unseen gun barrel erupted again, and again; then a third time. Each shot was farther from Mort. He watched the pattern in amazement. Jay evidently didn't know where Mort was, after all.

"Jay — cut it out. Listen to me, kid. Come out of there and go back to Clearwater with me. The doc'll patch you up."

"If I go back to town with you, Mort, it'll be tied across my saddle. And — I don't care whether I go like that or not, y'see? You've got Tassie. I've got nothing. Just two guns and a shell-belt full of slugs — so come get me, Mort, if you want me to go back with you."

Mort picked up a pebble and threw it. Jay fired instantly at the sound. Mort shook his head and peered round for the tell-tale glint of gun metal. He didn't see it, and tossed in another rock. That time Jay fired with the throaty 45. It was a good shot, too; caught the rock while it was still rolling and blew it to bits.

Mort sat in silence, wondering whether to risk a close-in duel or not. He didn't have much more time, and knew it. The posse couldn't be far off now, even if they were riding slowly, which they'd had to do if they expected to ride the same horses back out of the desert again. He got up painfully and inched along the barrier of granite that hid him from his brother.

"You're coming, aren't you, Mort?"

Mort didn't answer; just kept inching along, trying to see a gun barrel in the blinding sunlight.

"Bang!"

It was close; too close. Mort flattened and lowered himself to the ground. Jay had caught a flash of movement or the sound of Mort's boots. Something, anyway; for he knew where Mort was.

"Missed me, Jay. You're a lousy shot."

Jay swore, but didn't fire again. "Keep wiggling around out there. I'll get you all right. Just keep moving, Mort. You'll see."

Mort crawled in a flanking direction. Each movement was agony, but there was a slight chance that he could get around his brother, and any movement was better than sitting there, frying alive among the scalded rocks. Mort's tongue was thickening, keeping pace with the dehydration of his body.

"Jay — this is the last time I'm going to try an' talk some sense into you. The last time I'll give you a chance to come out and go back to Clearwater with me."

"Save your breath. Shut up an' give me just one good crack at you. Anyway, Mort, you're wanted for murder, too. Wouldn't either of us get ten feet into town before we'd get lynched, now."

Mort drew in a long, unsteady breath. "You won't come out, Jay?"

"No!"

"S'long, Jay."

In reply to his final words Mort got livid abuse. It didn't phase him. He stood up again, and almost before the bend was out of his legs ducked low again at the sight of movement among the boulders off to his left.

Staring in consternation, he saw what he feared might happen. Walsh's possemen had come up, heard the shooting, evidently, and located the brothers by it; left their horses far back somewhere and sneaked up afoot. Mort's eyes narrowed tight against the sun's glare. He raked the land for more signs of lawmen, saw none, and pursed his lips. They were out there, all right — and hidden, waiting for either of the Ramsey brothers to show flesh. Mort was caught between two fires, as he'd known he might be. As Jay had said he'd be.

Swearing under his breath, Mort shinnied towards the up thrust jumble of rocks that marked the western barrier of Jay's natural fortress. It was slow going. He dared not show himself, front or rear. After what seemed a lifetime, he flattened against the baked earth and rested. Seconds later a voice called out that he'd come to recognise of late: Sheriff Walsh.

"Ramsey! Both of you! Come out of there with your — !"

Jay shot twice, fast. The sheriff bit off his words. Mort pressed tighter against the ground, waiting. Strangely enough, the sheriff's men didn't return the fire.

"Damn you! Which one of you did that?"

"Me," Jay bellowed. "And I've got a lot

more. Come on up and get 'em, lawman."

"You fool. You're surrounded. Come on out or get killed. You don't stand a Chinaman's chance."

"I'll come out," Jay called back, "when you pack me out."

"All right. That's just what we'll do. That's what we're here for. Is Mort in there with you?"

"No; the dirty skunk's around in front of me somewhere."

Walsh's blistering oaths rang out among the rocks. "Mort? Come out. Come on out of there, boy."

Mort groaned quietly. If he'd wanted to give himself up he dared not. "Can't, Sheriff. Jay's too close, and you're behind me."

"We won't shoot," Walsh called back.

"Maybe not," Mort answered drily, "but Jay will as soon's I stand up."

And Jay did, guessing Mort's position from the sound of his voice. He cursed Mort again, aloud; then the sheriff broke in with some scathing comments of his own, and hailed Mort again.

"We dassen't shoot Mort, with you in there."

Mort's brows drew together in wonder. Why? What purpose did the sheriff have in refusing to fight him? He was going to call out and ask, but just at that moment Jay's wild laughter erupted again, and every man among the rocks who heard it looked towards a companion in wonder. Sheriff Walsh turned to the smaller, worried-looking man at his side.

"What a hell of a laugh, Doc!"

"He's out of his head, Sheriff. I wondered if he mightn't be when I first heard him. Listen — get Morton Ramsey out of there some way."

Walsh shook his head like an angry bull, flinging sweat off his chin. "Well — damn it — you got any more bright ideas? Mort can't come out with his brother laying for him back there."

"But you promised to —"

Walsh swore and made a helpless gesture with his gunhand. "I know that. I said *if* I could salvage him alive; not that I would. Listen to me, Doc: this is the law's affair. If you want a cholera prospect, you'll have to wait until this is over with. Damn it all, man. You can tell if he's got it easier dead than alive, anyway, can't you?"

The doctor turned wrathfully. "Sheriff — I'm warning you. *That man must be taken alive!*"

Walsh's face purpled all over again. "Are

you ordering me to — ?"

"That's exactly what I'm doing. Ordering you to take Morton Ramsey alive. And I'll go further, too. I'll promise you a Federal investigation of your conduct in this mess, if you don't take him alive. How d'you suppose the United States Marshal'll like hearing how you went to sleep like a kid, and let Ramsey walk out of your jailhouse?"

Walsh winced. "Dammit, Doc. Aw — why don't you make your tests on his corpse? It'll be just as plain, won't it?"

The doctor turned back to his squinteyed study of the fugitive's hiding place. When he spoke it was in the same tone of voice he'd use in explaining something to a child. "Listen, Sheriff: it isn't the tests I'm worried about. If you kill Morton Ramsey we'll never know who's been in contact with him since he broke out of your jail; and unless we know that — if he *has* the cholera — we won't have any way to isolate the people who might spread the damned disease. *Now* do you understand why he's got to be taken alive?"

Walsh didn't answer. If he was going to he never got the chance. A carbine shot blasted aside the brief lull. Walsh ducked instinctively like everyone else did. But the slug had come from Jay's hideout. Mort had risked a slight movement towards the possemen; drew no fire from that direction, and got to his knees. Instantly, Jay had fired. The bullet crashed into a rock inches from Mort's shoulders and forced him flat again. Jay had Mort pinned down. He gathered up a fistful of pebbles and flung them angrily towards Jay's position, and rolled desperately towards the last large boulder that separated him from his brother. Jay's fusillade was harmless, and Mort lay on his stomach panting and locking his teeth against the pain in his body, aware that he had no retreat and the only way for him to survive the unequal duel was to get around Jay some way and shoot him. There was no longer any alternative. Still puzzled by the law's unwillingness to fight him, he was thankful for it nevertheless.

The heat was nearly unbearable as Mort left his carbine in the dust and pulled out his .45, cocked it and inched forward, holding his breath. Scant inches separated him from a sweeping vision of Jay's hideout. He let his breath out very slowly and pushed the pistol barrel around the last boulder. If Jay saw it — and Mort suspected that he had — then he was waiting for an arm to show before he fired. Jay had known where Mort was when he'd yelled to Walsh. Then he must have guessed Mort's course and purpose.

Mort licked his lips and poked the cocked hand-gun farther out, waiting a terrible moment; then gave a hard push with one boot-sole against a granite boulder. The sudden movement catapulted Mort's head and shoulders into view around the rocky barricade. He caught a flash of movement and fired instinctively at it. Seconds later Jay's carbine roared. Mort tugged back the dog and let off his second shot, but he was moving, rolling, when he fired. Neither shot found the target.

Jay fired once more with the carbine, then dropped the gun, leaped frantically into a rocky crevice and slashed downwards with talon-like fingers for the .45 in his hip holster. Mort saw his own peril instantly and leaped erect, ducked back to the inner wall of the natural parapet and flattened against it. Jay would have to expose himself at least sideways to fire around the lip of stone that protected him.

Mort moved forward, determined to end the fight quickly. His body was raked with burning pain. The nausea was rising within him again. He fought off the accompanying giddiness and inched forward in a sideways, crab-like crouch.

"Mort? Mort?" It was Jay again. The voice was thick and unsteady now. "Step out into the open. I'll face you man to man. I'll —"

Mort fired at the lip of rock, saw the splinters fly and heard Jay's voice break off so abruptly that the silence that followed was louder than the voice had been. He didn't answer at all. Didn't have to. They were so close now that any movement Jay made would precipitate death for one — probably both — of them.

Then the minutes of waiting began to drag themselves through the leaden, stifling atmosphere. Mort wouldn't step around Jay's barrier. To do so would be instant death. Jay wouldn't come out, either. Mort's shot had shown the killer the folly of facing his brother. Impasse again. Mort ignored the salt-sweat that ran off him. Ignored the clawing pain in his hip and along the scored ribs. Forgot the thirst that was making his mouth taste like an alkali sink. Ignored everything, in fact, except the little ridge of upright rock that separated him from a remorseless killer.

And time went draggingly over the shriven land, scourged with heat, clubbed with anxiety and doubt, until the seconds seemed to be standing still. Mort waited,

185

close to exhaustion but with enough will to live not to step around the escarpment of granite and be killed by his brother, who couldn't miss at the distance.

Mort's surprise couldn't have been greater, then, when Walsh called out suddenly. He had completely forgotten the lawmen out in front, so absorbed had he been in the duel with Jay.

"Jay — you're bottled up, coming and going. This is absolutely your last chance. Come out with your guns holstered or we're coming in after you."

For a spell there was no answer; then, when it came, the voice was thin and barely recognisable to Mort. "You got my answer, Walsh. It's still the same. If I came out you'd hang me, anyway."

"That's not my job. That's up to a judge or a jury. I'm here to take you back to Clearwater. That's all I'm —"

"Yeah. I know. You might mean it, too; but Clearwater won't wait. They'll hang me, Walsh — I know they will. You think I'm a fool?"

"More than a fool," Walsh said, with meaning. "All right — you had your chance and didn't take it. Now I'm coming in after you!" Mort ground his teeth. Walsh was forcing his hand. Jay couldn't stay in his protective crevice much longer. Not with Walsh coming up on him from the south and Mort a scant few feet west of him. The showdown was near, and Mort's palms were sticky-moist and oily where the gun-butt lay. He edged in tighter against the lip of rock, seeking as much protection as he could get — which was none, really — should his brother jump backwards out of his rock-crack instead of going over the top of it in the face of the posse.

Pistols with their stentorian roar, and carbines with a flatter, more solid sound, smashed into the dead atmosphere like giant fists. Mort straightened up in surprise. Lead was careening all around him. A long, quavering yell arose over the fierce battle out beyond, then trailed off — only to rise again, punctuated by gun blasts. He stood the suspense until the first lull in the firing, then braced himself and moved as swiftly as he could around the lip of granite facing Jay's crevice. It was empty. The sun shone malignantly off innumerable carbine and six-gun casings, but Jay wasn't in the shelter at all.

Understanding came slowly, because it didn't make sense. Jay had wanted to kill Mort. Yet, in the final showdown, he hadn't leaped out to face his brother's gun but had gone over the top of his boulder fortress and charged against Sheriff Walsh's posse.

A little numb from the realisation of what had happened, Mort worked his way into the crevice and found footholds among the stone jumble; pulled himself up carefully, cautiously, and risked a peek, now that most of the firing was over. Two men lay sprawled across boulders that evidently had once shielded them. They were both face-down. L. C. Walsh — sparse hair damp and clinging, hat gone, and as rigid as a statue — with a stubby .45 in his right fist, was standing wide-legged on a flat rock, shooting down into a bare spot surrounded with rock rubble. He was obviously swapping shots with someone down in the depression, beyond Mort's vision. It would be Jay — and if Jay was down there it meant he was too badly hit to run any farther.

Mort pulled himself over the top of the parapet and shouted at Walsh, but the racket was still too loud for his words to carry. When he was drawing-in another deep breath to cry out again, the last of the firing stopped as suddenly as it had started. Mort's mouth hung open. He was staring at the sheriff. Walsh was motionless, looking down into the opening in the rocks intently. Slowly, very methodically, he brought his gaze to bear on the gun in his hand, lifted it, and began to reload it — never once glancing down at the man who had shot it out with him, after that single, long stare.

Mort saw others appear here and there among the rocks. Watched as they came up, necks craned and guns ready. Then he began the treacherous trek across the boulders to where Walsh was standing. Close enough, Mort veered off a little, went over and glanced down at what he knew would be sprawled down there. He was right. Jay lay on his back, legs crumpled under him, one arm flung over some small stones. The other — his gun hand — was being supported by the doctor.

"Mort — come here a minute."

He looked up and saw that Walsh was regarding him stonily. "It's all over, boy. Doc's with Jay. Come here."

Mort made no move towards the sheriff. He saw the grey exhaustion in the lawman's face and felt that he must look worse. Walsh didn't repeat the order when he spoke again.

"What happened back there? How come him to charge the whole damned posse?"

Mort slumped a little, feeling the heat burning into his back through his shirt. "I don't know. We were only a couple of feet apart when he went over the top and tried to shoot it out with you fellers. Must've been crazy. It doesn't make sense to me."

"No?" Walsh said quietly, holstering his gun and reaching down for his hat. He regarded a bullet-hole through the crown critically, then shrugged and pulled the hat on with a careless tug. "Well, I'll tell you one thing — two things, in fact. One is that Jay was out of his head. Doc said so. He told me while we were lyin' behind those rocks that Jay wasn't acting rational at all."

Mort spoke without looking at Walsh. "I guessed that, long before you fellers showed up. Guessed it after I got up here and talked to him."

"Doc said it might be sunstroke. Maybe your shot alongside the head shook up his internal workings some way." The sheriff shrugged. "Well — he's gone. We'll never know, I don't reckon. Doesn't make much difference, anyway."

"What was the other thing you were going to tell me?"

"Jay died game. Crazy, maybe; but game. How many times did he get a shot at you before we came up? I counted three, myself."

Mort shrugged. "I don't know; plenty though. Why?"

"Well — Doc said he was damned near blind when he came over the top of the rocks. He was actin' funny, the way he ran. I asked Doc about it. He was watching Jay coming at us with his damned gun blazing away just like it was a medical problem. I had to yank Doc back twice, then he told me to watch your brother's shooting. I did. You know what he was doing? Shooting blind; spraying lead! He downed two Clearwater boys that were sixty feet to the right of him, an' he wasn't chargin' straight at us at all. He was so near to bein' blind, Mort, that he didn't know for sure where we were. When he fired, it was at a sound, not a sight. That's how come him to get those two boys way over on the right. They were scramblin' in the rocks; weren't even firin' at him. Those of us who didn't move and yet were in plain sight he never even shot at."

Mort had the answer to the way Jay had been acting and shooting since Mort had first come up. At the time he had wondered, too, but hadn't had time to think much about it, either, for the posse had crept up and all hell had broken loose after that. He was standing, hip-shot, staring at the ground, when the doctor scrambled up out of the rocky depression where his brother lay, stopped at sight of Mort and stuffed a limp piece of paper into a baggy coat pocket.

"Mort: he's not quite done yet. You might want to sit with him. . . ."

Mort looked at the sheriff. "I thought you said he was . . . ?"

"Made a mistake, I reckon." He turned towards the doctor as soon as Mort began the sliding descent into Jay Ramsey's hole in the rocks. "You get it, Doc?"

"Yes, but it's pretty weak-looking. Scrawled, is about all you can say for it."

"We don't give a damn about that, just so's you got it."

"I did."

"Keep it until we need it, and go over and see to those two boys who got hit, will you?"

The doctor clambered over the rocks again without saying anything. The rest of the possemen were clustered around the downed men. Walsh looked thoughtfully down at the Ramsey brothers, then turned on his heel and headed towards the other group, where the doctor was elbowing his way towards two still, bloody bodies stretched out in the shade.

Mort heard Walsh's boot-heels crunching overhead and didn't look up. "Jay? Can you hear me all right?"

"Yeah. It's Mort — isn't it?" The strained

sound was gone out of the dying man's voice now. He sounded very weak and lethargically tired.

"Yeah, it's Mort, Jay. Why didn't you come after me? You stood at least an even break that way. You or me."

Jay's bandage was askew. His face was chalky white and blood ran down his neck from beneath the bandage near his left ear. "No secret now, Mort. I couldn't see good enough. Something went wrong with my eyes soon's I left the forest and hit out over this damned desert. Maybe the bandage wasn't as good as a hat; I don't know. Mort? Everyone makes 'em — I've made mine. I'm not sorry. Mort . . . ?"

"Yes, Jay?"

But Jay didn't answer him: the sheriff did. He was standing above them, looking down again. "That's it, Mort. He's gone." Walsh said it quietly but with neither pity nor compassion in his voice. He was simply stating a fact. Jay Ramsey was dead.

Mort got up and started to walk. He didn't look round at the faces that followed him as he found Pat Reilly's black stallion, clawed his way into the saddle and headed towards Clearwater with his head low on his chest. Walsh watched him for a moment, then beckoned-up two grimy-faced, villain-

193

ous-looking possemen and pointed.

"That's Mort Ramsey. He's half delirious. Doesn't even remember he's wanted for murder. Herd him along, boys. Those Ramseys're a tough breed. They c'n be dyin' and still get up an' ride away. Just sort of mind him. I think he's goin' to town anyway, but follow along an' make sure."

The men trotted to their horses, stepped up and struck out behind Mort in a shambling trot. Walsh watched the trio from where he stood, shook his head and turned when the medical man climbed up on to the flat rock and touched his arm.

"One's creased along the jaw; the other's got a badly shattered shoulder. They'll both live, I think."

"That so?" the sheriff said absently, casting a final look after the gaunt scarecrows on spent, listless horses that were heading towards Clearwater, one far in the lead on a black stallion. "Let's get back then." He turned away from the doctor and jerked a calloused thumb towards Jay Ramsey. "Couple you boys tie him across a saddle and head for town. Rest of you fix up some blanket slings for our wounded there, then let's get back where there's some drinking water."

Mort had forgotten Walsh and his posse

completely. What his thoughts were, exactly, he never could recall. He was heading back towards town all right; but that must have been an instinct, because he didn't quite make it. He was still three miles out when the two men who had been detailed to watch him saw the black stud-horse begin to wander off the trail erratically. They rode up quickly but not in time to catch the stallion's rider. Mort sagged, went lower and finally fell off the left side of the animal with a fluid, gentle sort of motion that indicated he was unconscious before he cleared the saddle. The possemen sat there staring at him, then one of them — a man with blood-shot eyes and lips like a bear-trap — grunted down off his mount.

"Man's carcass'll just stand so much. Gimme a hand, Al. We'll tie him up there and kind of steady him into town."

So Morton Ramsey came back to Clearwater astride after all — but more dead than alive. People stopped and stared. No one hollered to the grimy, sun-blackened possemen until they were tying up before Walsh's office, then several cow-boys came across the roadway and helped the two men carry Mort into Walsh's office. They put him in the same wall-cot, backed off a little and stood mutely staring down at him. They were like that when the sheriff walked in, threw them a cold nod and spoke past cracked lips.

"All right, boys — thanks."

The dismissal was abrupt and final. The riders left, taking the two bedraggled possemen with them and heading for one of the saloons, where the phlegm they'd picked up on the wilderness road and beyond it, at Dead Water, could be cut by strong liquor.

Walsh watched the doctor cross the room and bend low over Mort. "Now what, Doc? He's been close to about half the menfolk of Paiute Valley."

The medical man shook his head slowly in silence, probed at Mort's flesh, rolled back his eyelids and pulled up a little stool and sat on it, without looking back at the sheriff at all.

"Lord: how can a body stand all that?"

Walsh was making a cigarette. He had dumped his hat on the floor beside the chair he sat in, and was feeling the dull ache in his heat-swollen feet. "It can't," he answered. "He told me the Ramseys're a tough breed when I had him in here before. I figured he was talking through his hat. Well — I made a mistake. They're tough all right, like boiled owls. Tough and blind-stubborn." The smoke curled up past Walsh's grey-weary face. His frosty eyes went to Mort's features and stayed there. "You reckon he'll make it this time, Doc?"

The doctor was making new bandages. He twisted on the stool and wagged his head slowly back and forth. "If he does, no one'll be more amazed than I will."

"If he doesn't — my fine Christian friend — you'll be a week or so longer trying to figure out whether he had cholera and passed it around, too."

The medical man grunted and turned back to his bandage making. "That's a fact," he said glumly.

"Well — can't you tell by now whether he has it or not?"

"How?" the doctor demanded irritably. "He's burning-up with fever from exposure, loss of blood, physical exhaustion and a dozen other things — and unconscious on top of that."

"Hell," Walsh said defensively, "I just asked." He recalled something the doctor had said to him only the day, before. "That's your department, Doc."

"Well," the medical man snapped right back, "I don't have a crystal ball, y'know. I can't do the impossible."

"You ought to get one, then," Walsh said, rising; wincing from the pain in his feet and smiling oddly. "That's what Mort told me once. I'll pass it along to you."

"Where are you going?"

"To get a drink. Want me to send you over one?"

"Yes, if you will. A double shot of bourbon."

The sheriff went across the roadway, shook off several hands that would have detained him, went into the Last Chance Saloon, had one fast drink and left orders for someone to take the double bourbon over to the doctor, then went back out into the smashing heat and ambled aimlessly south to the first side-street. His mind was working smoothly in spite of the bone-weariness that made every movement an effort instead of an instinct.

At the Clement household one roll of knuckles across the door brought Tassie to the opening. Walsh looked at her face, then shifted his glance beyond, to the cool interior of the house.

"Well — can I come in?"

"I'm sorry, Sheriff. Please. . . ." She held the door open. He went past her, saw the leather rocker in a shadowy corner and went for it like a bull busting towards a thicket in fly-time.

"Sheriff?"

He sat down gingerly, extended his legs and looked dourly at the boots encasing his swollen feet. "Let me tell it my way, Tassie."

She stood by, watching him. Seeing the utter weariness and stubborn refusal to be rushed or influenced, both.

"Sit down, girl. Makes my feet hurt watching you stand there."

She crossed the room and sat down on the edge of a horsehair sofa, facing him. He flashed another fleeting glance at her face, saw the same unnerving anguish there, and looked down at his boots again.

"Mort's alive and Jay's dead." She didn't move and he didn't look up. "Jay was hiding out at the Pat Reilly place. Some way or another Mort figured it like that and rode out there. That was after he clouted me, of course. Carrie Reilly gave us the story. We trailed Mort, who was trailing his brother. Jay made it to Dead Water and forted up. Mort was between us, but I told the boys to hold off until Mort had a chance."

Tassie spoke quickly, unable to hold it back any longer. "Was Mort hurt — again — Sheriff?"

"Well — he wasn't shot again. Jay probably couldn't find a spot to put another slug. No; he wasn't hit again, Tassie, but he's in pretty bad shape."

"I'll go over and see him."

"No," Walsh said quickly. "Not just yet. Let the sawbones work his mumbo-jumbo, first. In a little while, maybe. I'll let you know."

"But — is he . . . ?" She let it trail off.

Walsh pulled down his mouth. "You ought to know better'n ask a thing like that. This isn't the time or the place. Anyway — how would I know? How would anyone know? Time'll tell — that's all. He's pretty bad off. Exposure, fever, wounds and all." The hard eyes lifted to the girl's face. "I'm no pill roller, but I've got an idea that most of Mort's serious hurts are inside, not out-side. I want you to see him as soon as I can get you in there. This is just an idea of mine, but I reckon he needs your kind of patching up more'n he needs doc's kind."

"I'll go right now; any time — just let —"

"I know you will. I'll keep watch for you. May even have to sneak you in there, so don't say anything to anybody about it."

"I won't. Sheriff — we owe you a lot."

Walsh looked up quickly, the hardness in his glance again.

"You owe me nothing. I'm not doing a darned thing I shouldn't do. Just keep it under your hat — that's all."

Tassie nodded. "And — Jay — Sheriff?"

"I was coming to that. Jay wasn't right in the head out there. Out at Dead Water. Doc said he might've been sunstruck or it might've been Mort's bullet alongside his skull. He acted crazy and Doc said he thought he was. But he's dead. Anyway — I don't think that's what shook-up Mort so much. It was bound to jolt him, knowing he was fighting a brother of his own — and one that wasn't right in the head."

"What else was it, Sheriff?"

"Jay was darned near blind. I don't reckon it occurred to Mort that he was, though, when they were fighting. Mort wasn't in too good a shape himself, remember."

"Jay — blind?"

"Yeah. Doc and I rode back to town to-gether. He explained it like this. Mort's slug may have barely nicked some optic nerve, y'see; and then, what Jay's carbine didn't finish with its jolting, the sun may have done. Anyway, he could see sort of hazy like, Doc said. Make out outlines and the like, but he couldn't tell much unless there was movement." Walsh exhaled wearily and moved his sore feet a little.

"And when the showdown came, Tassie, he didn't shoot it out with Mort after all. We'll never know why he didn't, but I've got an idea on that. No man's all bad. Not even the worst ones. And Jay was a bad one all right. Nope; in the showdown he let Mort live and came out of his hole in the rocks like a catamount. Charged blind into my posse. Jay had a hate worse than Mort. It was the law." The blue eyes raised and stayed on Tassie's face.

"Mort didn't shoot his brother: I did. I'm neither proud of it nor ashamed of it. It's one of those things that men have to do. Lawmen, anyway."

Somewhere in the back of the house a wall clock with a big brass pendulum ticked unconcernedly, monotonously, keeping the silence from becoming more oppressive than it was. Tassie and the sheriff sat in the parlour looking at one another and saying nothing. Walsh gripped the arms of the rocker and pushed himself upwards.

"Any questions, Tassie? I'm going to get about twenty-four hours of sleep, so if you've got anything that needs answering right now, better get it out."

She rose, facing him. "When will the doctor be sure about Mort?"

"Oh, I'd say by tomorrow, maybe. You'd have to see him on that." A dull sparkle of irony showed in Walsh's eyes. "That's his department."

"And — what about Jay?"

Walsh moved to the door, grasped the latch and lifted it.

"You and Mort can juggle that one between you. We brought him in; he's in the dead-shed behind doc's house."

He turned thoughtfully. "Might be a good idea to plant him quick, though — it's pretty darned hot this time of the year. Tell doc I said you can have the remains, if you see him before I do. Where'll you bury him?"

"I don't know," Tassie said simply. "He was Mort's brother."

"Yeah. Well — don't wait too long or Doc'll stick him up in boothill."

"I won't, Sheriff; and thank you so very much for all you've done. I — don't know what else to say. You've been —"

"Never mind that," Walsh butted-in swiftly. "I get my thanks in cash from the city fathers once a month. It's just a job to me."

Tassie watched him go down the plankwalk towards the centre of town. She stood in the doorway for several minutes, then softly closed out the broiling sunlight, went back over to the sofa and sat on the edge of it again; closed her eyes and didn't move at all for five minutes. A prayer might not help, but no one was ever injured by one, either.

After that she went outside and walked steadily down to the doctor's combination home and office, accepted the sympathetic smile of the medical man's wife — whom everyone in Clearwater, young and old alike, called "Aunt Emily" — and saw the doctor's harassed look across the parlour from her. He was looking up from a scrap of dingy paper that he'd spread carefully on his desk. Regarding her with an air of quizzical expectancy, he nodded.

"How is Mort, Doctor?"

"How is he? Well, as good as can be expected, I'd say. Sit down, Tassie." He threw his wife a quick, knowing look. "Could we have some root beer, Emily?"

Tassie sat. It was apparent to the doctor that she was holding herself in with great restraint. He folded the little paper carefully, placed it back in his wallet, turned fully on the chair and faced the girl.

"Did you ever have a drink of bourbon, Tassie?"

"Once. A sip out of my father's glass. It's terrible."

"Yes — well — you need one now. I'll pour you just a wee dram into your root beer. All right?"

"All right."

He poured it from a dark bottle in one of

204

the cramped drawers on his desk, saw the look his wife threw him, ignored it and handed the glass to Tassie.

"It'll be tasteless that way."

It was. She was surprised to find that the root beer had diluted the tartness. It didn't take long for it to work through Tassie, either, and until it did she sat there like a small bird about to take wing. Then she relaxed. A lot of the tension faded from her face. Even the look in her eyes was calmer.

"Will he live, Doctor?"

The doctor shrugged. "Only the Lord knows the answer to that one, and He won't say. I don't like to commit myself in cases like this."

"Is he that bad?" Her eyes grew enormous in the sudden stillness of her face.

"He's plenty bad, I'm afraid. Right now it's fever; shock and inertia — all combined. When I left him he was —"

"You left him — alone?"

"He's not alone. Manuel from the beanery next door is there. He's to call me if Mort comes round."

A slow flush was climbing into her cheeks. "I'll go over and —"

"I'm sorry," the doctor said hastily, almost sharply, "but you can't. Not for a while."

"Why not?"

"Well — he shouldn't be disturbed."

"I won't disturb him. I'll just sit there. Be there in case he needs anything."

"I'm sorry, Tassie; he can't have visitors yet. Don't worry — I'm watching him like a hawk."

Her colour was two shades brighter than normal. She stood up quickly. "Excuse me, Doctor, but you can't keep a very good watch from here. I'm going over there to be with him."

The doctor jumped up quickly, consternation bringing up his own colour. "Tassie — you can't!"

She went towards the door, and her answer went back to him over her shoulder. "I can — and I will!"

He watched the door close behind her. Stood in shock for a moment, then snatched up his hat, clapped it over the bushy grey hair and loped out after her. But Tassie was already hurrying towards the jail. She'd be in there before he could head her off. Biting his underlip, the doctor headed for the sheriff's house in a shuffling trot that brought him to the door in short order. One urgent knock, and Peggy Walsh, the sheriff's wife, was facing him.

"Miz Walsh — I've got to see L.C. right away."

"He's resting, Doctor. Perhaps I could — ?"

"I've got to see him — now!"

"Well — he's resting. He was awfully tired when he came in."

"I know, Ma'am," the doctor said wryly. "I was out at Dead Water with him; but this won't wait."

The sheriff's wife stepped aside doubtfully and watched the doctor scuttle into the lawman's bedroom and disappear. She was braced for what she knew would come — and it came.

"Now listen, Doc — dammit — there's a time and place for everything."

"Hold on a minute, L.C. Tassie Clement went over to your jailhouse to sit with Mort. She'll be exposed."

The sheriff ran a hand through his thinning hair and motioned towards a sack of tobacco hanging by its strings to a chair where his shirt and shell-belt were. "Hand me that sack, Doc."

The doctor complied, then launched into a tirade about the dangers of a cholera epidemic. Walsh made his cigarette, lit it, exhaled and fixed the medical man with a cold, unperturbed glance.

"Hold up a second, Doc. Mort's exposed about two-thirds of the people around here, anyway. He's been lugged in and out of my office at least twice. He's been breathing the same air as I have off and on for a week now. He's been —"

"I know all that. It doesn't alter the fact that we're honour bound to take every precaution we can. Cholera's a terrible —"

"And I," said the sheriff disgustedly, "have heard all this about ten times in the last week or so. Doc — I don't think he has it. If he *did* have, he'd have given it to me and all those other —"

"You're wrong, L.C. Maybe he doesn't have it, but it's still our job to make sure. The chance that —"

"Quit worrying, will you? Those Ramseys're the toughest breed of dogs I ever saw walk on their hind legs, believe me. If he has it — then so do I and a whale of a lot of other people. If he doesn't — which I'm inclined to believe is the case — then — doggone your hide — you ought to go home and take a long nap, like I'm doing. In either case — *get t'hell out of here and let me sleep!*"

"What about the girl? What about Tassie Clement?"

"What about her? You mean she's in there with him? Well — I think she's just exactly the medicine he needs: more than your doggoned pills and horse liniment. That answer your question?"

"No, dammit, it doesn't. She'll have to be isolated too, now."

"Huh! I don't reckon she'll object to that," Walsh said drily.

"But her folks'll have to know. The story'll spread. There'll be a panic as sure as you're a foot high."

The sheriff looked at the red tip of his cigarette for a second, then shot a wrathy look at the doctor. "All right — all right. I'll arrest her again. Make her stay in the jailhouse. Now are you satisfied enough to go home and go to sleep like a sensible man ought to?"

The doctor turned it over in his mind, found it acceptable, and stood up. "All right, L.C. See you later."

"You sure will. Bust in here once more and you'll see me all over you, like one of those damned rashes you're always worrying about." Walsh punched out his cigarette and listened to the front door close, cocked his head when Mrs. Walsh appeared in the doorway, and glowered at her.

"Don't you ever let that pipsqueak in here again when I'm in bed, or I'll —"

"Or what — L.C.?"

The sheriff stared at her a moment, then turned on his side and muffled whatever he had wanted to say into the pillow, while he punched it to fit his shoulders and tried once more to get some sleep.

But the implications behind the doctor's words, plus his obvious fright, nibbled at the edges of the sheriff's mind so that sleep wouldn't come. He tossed and swore for a listless half-hour, then shoved off the bed, dressed, buckled on his shell-belt and went, stamping out of the house and down the plank-walk towards his office. Tassie was putting a damp rag over Mort's forehead when Walsh entered the office and glared at her.

"Tassie: you're under arrest as an accessory to Mort's damned monkeyshines. You can't leave this jail until the doc says you can."

Tassie's eyes were round in astonishment. "The doctor, Sheriff? Why him?"

"I didn't mean that. I — was thinking of something else. I meant until *I* say you can. You understand?"

"Yes," she said meekly, turning back to Mort. "I'm glad — because I wouldn't have left, anyway. There's just one thing, Sheriff."

"Now what?"

"Since I can't leave here — would you go down to the doctor's and ask him to make the arrangements for Jay's funeral? We —

Mort and I — want him to have a decent burial. Not in boothill, Sheriff. Over in the town cemetery. A nice casket and all. Will you do that for us?"

Walsh groaned aloud. "I don't want to see that little pipsqueak —"

"But I'm under arrest," Tassie said demurely. "I can't be walking around Clearwater — can I?"

Walsh's neck got turkey-red but he managed, through heroic effort, to stem the profanity that came unbidden behind his damped teeth.

"Please — Sheriff?"

Walsh didn't answer. He turned and slammed the door behind himself, glared at the man he'd stationed outside to keep curious townsmen away, and stalked angrily towards the doctor's house. Halfway there, the tangy, inviting aroma of a saloon detoured him. Inside the big room, with its musty smell and atmosphere of masculinity, he felt the indignation that was in him soften a little.

"Whisky, Sheriff?"

"Naw; ale."

The barman drew the tankard and slid it deftly in front of the lawman. "Excitement's about over now, huh?"

"If you mean the Ramseys — no — it

211

isn't. There's to be a funeral for one and a trial for the other." He downed the ale, had another one, paid for them both and went back outside again, dragging a sleeve across his mouth.

At the doctor's place he was stopped on the threshold by "Aunt Emily." They exchanged greetings, then Walsh asked to see the medical man.

"Sorry, Sheriff. He's asleep."

Walsh blinked, hard. "Well — I want to see him, anyway."

"Not now. Come back later. He's had a bad time of it these last twenty-four hours."

Walsh snorted loudly. *"He's* had a bad time of it! Where do you think I've been all this —"

"You're bigger," the doctor's wife said, with incomprehensible feminine logic. "He needs his sleep."

She closed the door in his face. Walsh stood aghast, staring at it for a long moment; then flung himself round and went stumping up the plank-walk again. The Last Chance Saloon loomed up in his line of march. He stopped, regarded the louvred doors, spat into the dusty roadway and went inside. The same barman nodded affably.

"Ale?"

"Naw, whisky. Rye whisky."

A look of mild surprise went over the barman's face. He shrugged and went to fetch the liquor. When he returned the sheriff was gone. Blinking, the barman put the glass down and stared at the louvred doors: they were still vibrating. Whatever had taken the sheriff away had done it fast.

CHAPTER SIX

A Matter of Murder

Tassie looked up, startled, when L.C. burst into the office. His glance flashed over Mort then back to the girl. "Tassie, when we were talking in here a little while ago, you said you and Mort had decided what to do with Jay. Do you mean to tell me he's conscious?"

"Yes, Sheriff. He's conscious. He came round shortly after I got here from the doctor's house."

Walsh crossed the room in four large steps, stood above the cot and stared. "Mort? Can you hear me?"

The answer was weak but distinct — and dry. "Can't help it, Sheriff. All Clearwater can hear you."

"Humph!" Walsh watched the blanched features. "Doc said you wouldn't be around for hours yet — if ever."

"Doc isn't always right, L.C.," Mort said quietly.

"No — I see that. How do you feel?"

"About like I look, I reckon."

"You couldn't feel that bad and be alive."

Walsh glanced at Tassie. "Would you — no, never mind — I'll do it."

"Do what, Sheriff?"

"Get that doggoned little pipsqueak of a pill-roller."

Mort heard the door slam behind the sheriff and moved his head the slightest bit. "Tassie? Do you want me to tell you the rest of it?"

She shook her head. "It isn't necessary, Mon. Sheriff Walsh told me when he came back from Dead Water."

"I'm glad," Mort said wearily, "I'd like to forget the whole darned thing for a while."

She didn't speak. His eyes roamed over the ceiling, down the walls, over the rough blankets that covered him and up to her face.

"Tassie? If a man asked you to marry him, what'd you say?"

"I'd say," she came right back, "that it'd depend on who the man was."

"Well — say it was one who deliberately made love to you and didn't mean it when he was doing it. Like, say, a man who thought you'd double-crossed him by sending the sheriff after him at Dead Water, and tried to repay you in kind. Not much of a man, the way I'm making him sound — is he?"

"I think he is," Tassie said. "If *that* man asked me to marry him, I'd say — yes."

He rolled his head and looked at her. "I'm that man. You understand that, don't you?"

"The answer is yes again, Mort. Yes, I know who the man is, and yes, I'll marry you."

Colour came into his face. His eyes sparkled. "Bend down, then. I'd like to kiss you again. My memory's not too good. Needs lots of reminders."

She bent quickly. He kissed her, felt his chapped, battered lips split with the effort and pressure, and bleed. It was a strange kiss. One that had more pain than pleasure in it. Afterwards they sat in silence for a while, and eventually Tassie struggled clear of her jumbled, breathless emotions, long enough to speak.

"Mort — they'll try you for the murder of Lem Cameron. You know that, don't you?"

"Yes."

"Do — you want me to get you — a gun?"

He looked up at her suddenly. "Tassie — you're all woman. You'd help me get out of here."

"So would a million other women. A woman in love, Mort —"

"I know. You told me that once before, remember? I haven't forgotten it."

"Well — do you? I can get one easily enough."

"No, honey. Listen: that'd only make it worse. I'm in trouble up to my ears, anyway. Besides, I decided to give up the day Jay shot me and pulled out afterwards. Running'd make an owlhoot of me for life. Before, I didn't care. Now, I do. You don't want to have to ride back-trails the rest of your life, and — raise our kids — to hate the law."

"I'd go with you, Mort," she said simply.

"I believe it, Tassie; but I won't ask you to."

"But, Mort — it's murder — not self-defence. You might get prison for life, or — hung."

"If I get one of those — well — then I'll have lost a bad gamble. There'll be lots of time after I lose — if I do — to make plans, Tassie; right now I'm hoping for all I'm worth."

"All right, Mort. I'll have dad send you over one of the stage company's lawyers."

"Don't bother, honey," Mort said. "I've got to do a little thinking first. Later, maybe; not now."

"We," she said. "Not 'I'."

Mort smiled at her. "You're powerful good medicine, lady. Kiss me — reckon I need another shot."

She was kissing him when Sheriff Walsh and the medical man entered the office. Walsh looked embarrassed, but the doctor brushed the thing aside. He walked over to the foot of the cot and gazed at Mort in impassive silence, then shook his head in utter disbelief.

"You can't be that well, Mort. It just isn't human."

"He's human all right, Doctor," Tassie said. "Very, very human."

"Amen." The doctor continued to regard Mort in absorbed silence, then he plunged both hands deep into his trousers pockets. "Mort? You have any cramps, internal pains or the like? Have any convulsions, or felt like you might have 'em?"

Mort looked up, bewildered. "No — I haven't had any of that stuff, Doc. Just feel a little weak, that's all." His glance whipped to the sheriff's face where Walsh was standing behind Tassie's chair. "Say — what the devil's wrong with you two?"

The doctor cleared his throat, glanced once, fast, at the sheriff, got no answering look and swung back to Mort. "Recollect an old gaffer you helped out back in the hills, who was sick?"

"Sure. L.C.'s brother. What about him?"

"Well, Mort: he had cholera. You were exposed to it. If you'd contracted it and spread it around there might have been a plague of the stuff in the country. It travels like wildfire, boy. That's the main reason I've been hounding L.C. to catch you and hold you."

Tassie was watching the doctor's face as he spoke. Understanding showed in her eyes. "That's why you didn't want me near him, isn't it?"

The doctor nodded. "That's right, Tassie. We wanted him isolated, even though he'd been running loose for the past few days. That's why L.C. arrested you and confined you here."

Mort's amazement had abated a little by then. "How about all the people I've been around? How about those riders who packed me in here both times, and the —"

The doctor's forehead was wrinkled when he interrupted. "I'll tell you frankly, Mort, that I was about frantic trying to figure out what to do. Seems like — shot-up and hunted down — you just wouldn't stay put. The implication was frightening — to me, at any rate."

"And now?" Mort asked, watching the doctor's face closely. "What do you think now?"

"I don't think you have it at all; but a few

more days of isolation wouldn't hurt — just to make doubly sure."

Walsh cleared his throat and looked up from a cigarette he was making. "He'll be isolated all right, Doc. You won't have to worry about that."

The doctor said nothing for a while, just looked over the bandages on Mort's tawny torso. "You're a tough breed, Mort. You'll pull through all right. I'm glad for you — and Tassie here."

Mort smiled. "Funny how things work out. I had no idea — in fact I'd just about forgotten helping-out that old feller up at the fringe of the forest." He screwed his eyes up a little. "Say — was that why L.C. tried so darned hard to take me alive at Dead Water? Wouldn't shoot at me at all?"

"Yeah," Walsh said through a cloud of smoke. "That's it exactly. Doc wanted the names of all the folks you might've exposed. Funny — that. If it hadn't been for that, Mort, I've an idea you'd be as dead right now as your brother is."

The doctor had a decided slope to his stance, like all the starch had suddenly leaked out of him. He turned towards the sheriff. "L.C.: how about me turning in? You don't need me any more and I need some rest."

The lawman shot a withering glance at the doctor. "By all means, my Christian friend, by all means. Never let it be said that *I* was rude enough to interrupt another man's rest."

The doctor's glance swung back to Tassie. "If he gets worse, or if anything happens, just send the law for me. *Adios* until tomorrow."

Walsh kicked up a stool and dropped on to it without even deigning to notice the doctor's exit. "Mort — I sent a rider for the Circuit Rider. He'll be here day after tomorrow to try you for the murder of Lem Cameron. You understand that's got to be done, don't you?"

There was something in the sheriff's words that didn't jibe with the facts at all. It sounded like Walsh was making a statement of routine facts, not warning Mort that his longevity was involved at all.

"Yeah; I understand." Mort felt Tassie groping for his hand. "I'd like to get it over with as soon as possible, too." He made a rueful face. "A thing like that hanging over a man's head is worse'n a lynch-rope."

"There'll be none o' that," Walsh said firmly. "I'll guarantee you that. Anyway, Clearwater's seeing things differently, now that the Camerons and their friends have left the country — one way or another." The sheriff eyed the end of his cigarette. "Murder's a serious thing, Mort."

"I know it is."

"Glad you understand that," the sheriff said, rising. "Reckon I ought to warn you the building's guarded outside all round."

Mort grinned in spite of himself. "I'm a little used-up for running out now, Sheriff."

"Yes, I suppose so — only I heard you say that once before, too."

"Don't worry, Sheriff. I won't even try it this time. I'm over my revenge now. The account's settled. All I want now is to face my trial and get it over with — one way or the other."

"That so? Then what?"

Mort shrugged. "That depends, Sheriff. One way, I'll be all washed up. The other way, I'll just be starting to live."

Walsh dropped his cigarette and stamped on it. He spoke without looking up right away. "That was a damn fool thing you did, Mort."

"Lem Cameron? I reckon it was, Sheriff. Did you ever see the best friend you ever had hung, just because he knew you? Well — I did. Pat Reilly turning at the end of a Cameron lynch-rope. This Lem Cameron jumped for me, I slugged him — then I cut

Pat down and hung Cameron in his place."

"Yeah," Walsh said drily. "Well — see you two later."

Tassie watched the door close behind the sheriff. "Sometimes I just hate him," she said, with feeling.

Mort's eyes were half closed in thought. "I'll bet you a good horse he's been like that all his life. Folks either like him or hate him — no in-betweens. He's pretty hard."

Tassie avoided Mort's glance. "I shouldn't feel like that, though. He's done us favours." She looked back at him. "I'm mixed up, I guess, darling."

"Don't blame you. Worst confusion you've been in yet was a little while ago when you said you'd marry me."

"No, that's not true. The worst thing I ever did was tell L.C. you were at Dead Water; but, Mort, I did it hoping — praying — he'd take you without a fight. I — loved you so much, Mort. I made him promise he wouldn't shoot you. That he'd make you surrender."

He looked at her gravely. "That might've been the worst thing, at that. I figured you'd told him — you knew that, didn't you?"

"Yes; I guessed it when you didn't come back after the fight with the Camerons. Otherwise — if you'd loved me like you said

— you wouldn't have gone off without me, no matter what you'd told me, Mort."

He didn't speak. They sat in absolute silence until the shadows grew long, each busy with their own thoughts; and both of them — while hiding it capably from the other — was gripped with fright over the trial that loomed with such sinister import on their individual horizons.

The days dragged, and Mort's strength returned startlingly, so that by the date of his trial he was able to walk — haltingly, it is true; but upright at any event. He was saved the necessity, however, when Sheriff Walsh came into the office and looked at them both.

"The Circuit Rider's decided to hold the court in here, Mort, so's you won't have to walk."

"Thanks," Mort said laconically. "Hope I don't keep you waiting at the gibbet, Sheriff."

"Mort!" Tassie was appalled.

Even Walsh fixed the indicted man with a fishy eye. "This is no time for being funny." He flagged a hand at Mort's naked chest. "You got a shirt? Wouldn't look right, being tried like that."

Tassie held up a new white shirt. The sheriff nodded and Mort moved so that she could slip it on him.

"Am I pretty enough to hang, honey?"

"Mort — please. . . ." She combed his unruly hair, with her lower lip caught between her small, even teeth. "Honey, can't I send for the lawyer? Dad's got him staying at the hotel across the road."

"I'd rather not, Tassie — unless it'd make you feel better."

"It would, Mort; a lot better."

"All right — only tell him to sit way in the back and keep quiet unless I call him up. Will you do that?"

"Yes."

Sheriff Walsh left the office for a short time, then returned with several strangers. Mort was introduced to the Circuit Rider, got a brusque nod, and watched the hawk-faced older man ensconce himself behind the sheriff's desk, spread out a saddlebag's contents of papers, pens and two dog-eared books, then lean back and stare back at Mort with frank curiosity.

Walsh cleared his throat. "Reckon we'd just as well begin, hadn't we, Judge?"

The Circuit Rider spoke to Mort. "I understand you are waiving a jury trial. Is that correct?"

"Yes," Mort said, feeling less confident as the seconds ticked by.

The judge nodded towards L.C. "I don't

see any reason for holding off, Sheriff." He turned towards one of the men who had accompanied him. "Bailiff!"

Oaths were given and the sheriff was seated first. The judge gazed at him calmly. "Sheriff Walsh — are you the man who cut down this Lem Cameron from the baulk of the Ramsey barn?"

"Yes, Your Honour. Me an' Tige Blackwell."

"Tell me, Sheriff, exactly what you saw."

"Lem hanging up there with his head sideways. We rode underneath and cut him down. Tige tossed — put — him across the back of his saddle and lugged him back to Clearwater."

"Was there any evidence of a struggle, Sheriff?"

"Not that I saw, Your Honour," Walsh said drily. "Lem'd been knocked over the head and dragged up. That's about all there was to it."

"No struggle, then?"

"No."

"And he was dead?"

Walsh looked in astonishment at the judge. "Yes; I just said —"

"The court is aware of what you said, Sheriff Walsh. Just answer the questions."

"Yes — Sir!"

"This Tige Blackwell: is he one of your deputies?"

"Yes, Sir."

"You may step down, Sheriff. Bailiff — call up Mister Tige Blackwell."

The deputy's face was shiny with perspiration. He rolled his hatbrim furtively between both hands.

"You're Deputy Sheriff Tige Blackwell?"

"Yes, Your High— Your Honour."

"What did you see the night you and Sheriff Walsh rode into the yard of the Ramsey ranch?"

"Lem Cameron hangin' in the barnyard."

"Anything else?"

"Didn't look for nothin' else, Your Honour."

"You then proceeded to cut Cameron down, in company with the Sheriff; is that right?"

"Well — Walsh made me shinny up the baulk and cut Lem down. He flopped like a turkey with its —"

"Confine yourself to answers only, Deputy."

"Yes, Your Honour."

"And, between you, you brought the cadaver back to Clearwater?"

"Well — we brought Lem's carcass back, but not between us. I had him flappin' behind my cantle all the way."

"Yes. Now — is there anything you'd like to add to your testimony?"

"Not much — 'cept Lem Cameron should've been hung five —"

"That's enough! Step down, and thank you."

Before the court could call another person to be questioned, a heavily-paunched man in a handsome, hard-top derby with rolled edges pushed into the room, made an apologetic little nod towards the judge and squeezed in towards the wall-bench, where he sat down. The judge eyed him, seemed to consider something, then lifted his eyebrows.

"Mr. Bennett?"

The heavily-built man rose instantly. He was freshly shaven and immaculate. "Your Honour?"

"Are you by any chance in this court in an official capacity?"

"Not exactly, Your Honour. I'm counsel for the Big Sink Stage Company. At the request of the vice-president I'm here should the defendant need legal representation."

The Circuit Rider turned towards Mort. His voice was as dry as cornsilk in a light breeze. Apparently he had reason to know the stage line's attorney well enough.

"Mister Ramsey — do you wish the stage company's attorney to represent you?"

"No, Your Honour. I may need advice, but I haven't asked for it yet."

The judge turned back to the bailiff. "Swear in the defendant."

Mort was sworn in, although he didn't understand a word of the verbal barrage fired at him by the bailiff, who was writing with one hand and attending to the swearing with the other hand.

"Mister Ramsey — give the court your version of the charge that's against you."

"May I ask two questions first, Your Honour?"

The judge considered, then nodded. "I reckon so. Do you want to question someone?"

"Yes, Sir: Deputy Tige Blackwell, then Sheriff L. C. Walsh."

The Circuit Rider leaned back and nodded. "Have at him, Mister Ramsey."

Mort turned his head, very conscious of the ring of eyes that were following his movements. "Deputy Blackwell — you and Sheriff Walsh cut Lem Cameron down, didn't you?"

"We did — Sir."

"And you two were the only ones in the yard at the time you cut him down, weren't you?"

"I reckon — I mean — yes, we were the only ones. The rest of the posse had gone —"

"There wasn't another living soul in that yard, was there?"

"No. I already told you —"

"Thanks, Deputy Blackwell." Mort faced the judge. "Sheriff Walsh next, Your Honour?"

His Honour was looking at Mort closely. He sat up in his chair and nodded. "The sheriff's your witness, Mister Ramsey."

Mort turned back, saw Walsh eyeing him furtively with a long frown, and spoke directly to him. "Sheriff — do you agree with your deputy that you and he were the only living men in the ranch yard when you cut Lem Cameron down?"

"Yes. If there was anyone else I didn't see 'em."

Mort turned back towards the judge. "Your Honour, I'm no lawyer. I'm not even a good arguer. Being a single man I've never had occasion to learn to argue — but I'd like to ask the court one question."

The judge was leaning forward, nodding his head a little. "You are at liberty to do so, Mister Ramsey. What is it?"

"How can you try a man for a crime no one saw him commit? That he has never admitted committing, and that there's no actual proof or witnesses that he *did* commit?"

The judge didn't move for several seconds. Then, very slowly, he swung his shaggy head towards the sheriff, gazed at him fixedly and lifted his eyebrows before he spoke. "Sheriff Walsh, the defendant wants to know why he's being tried. Will you so inform him?"

Walsh was sitting there dumbfounded. He cleared his throat, squirmed in his chair and continued to stare. The judge's glance grew stormy.

"Sheriff!"

Walsh started in his chair, squirmed once more, then made a protective gesture with one hand. "Well — hell — Mort. You know you hung Lem."

The judge's interruption was deceptively mild. It belied the look in his eyes. "Sheriff Walsh, this court wasn't convened to discuss what someone suspects — it wants proof. Sufficient proof to warrant trying a man on a charge of murder, with the possible penalty of death being the verdict." His Honour paused, let his words sink in, then went on: "Sheriff Walsh — will you please answer Mister Ramsey's question?"

"Yes — Your Honour." But he didn't. The words wouldn't come. The judge leaned back and fixed the sheriff with a lethal stare.

"Sheriff Walsh, tell this court exactly how you came to summon it to listen to this case. Precisely what are your charges based upon, and what proof have you in each instance?"

"Well — Your Honour — Mort never *denied* killing Lem Cameron."

"How long have you been a lawman, Sheriff?"

"Seventeen years."

"And in that time you've gone through this process of trial approximately how many times?"

"Hundreds, I reckon, but —"

"Then you know the procedure pretty well, don't you?"

"Yes, Your Honour."

The judge's face gathered colour as he strove for self-control. "Then how in hell, Sheriff, did you happen to call me all the way from the county seat to try a man who hasn't admitted committing a crime, and how is it you don't have any proof that he *did* commit a crime?"

"Well — Your Honour — I'll be damned if I know. It's been a snarl right from the start. First I'd have a prisoner, then I wouldn't have one. Then I had two of 'em, guilty as all hell, then they — escaped —

and got shot down. Then I had a girl in jail who wasn't really involved in the case — well, hardly — then I didn't, and now — now —"

"Yes, Sheriff? And now?"

"And now I reckon I went and forgot to get the confession from Mort here. It's been a hell of a —"

The judge groaned aloud and struck the desk-top with his open palm. Even the bailiff looked angry. The judge turned and faced Mort.

"Mister Ramsey — because of wanton dereliction of duty, you stand a free man. This court — no court, damn it — has the power to try you, let alone convict you of any crime that can't be proven against you."

"Your Honour," Mort said suddenly. "It's always been my intention to give L.C. a signed confession. Seems that every time we meet — well — I've usually had a gun in my hand, and I can't write with the empty one." The room erupted into laughter until His Honour glowered. "Or else," Mort went on, "I'm flat on my back and can't write at all. But I'll give the sheriff the confession any time he asks for it."

Flabbergasted, the judge stared. "You will?"

"Yes, Sir."

"You'll admit before this court that you single-handedly lynched this Lem Cameron?"

"Mort!" The cry was so shrill everyone started. Mort turned and looked at Tassie. She was standing up, rigid, staring at him. "Don't say that. Mort — you're hanging yourself. Darling — please. . . ." In desperation she turned to the stage company's lawyer. "Mister Bennett — tell him not to say any more."

Bennett was standing. The rest of the room was motionless with tension. Mort motioned the stage company lawyer away. His voice was the only calm one in the drama-packed room.

"Tassie, I don't aim to hide anything. You wouldn't want it that way for a lifetime. Yeah: I know you'll say you would; but really, honey, you wouldn't. Not five or ten years from now." He turned back towards the judge, ignoring the stares of the spectators, and spoke directly to the Circuit Rider.

"Your Honour, I strung Lem Cameron up after he jumped me in a fight and I slugged him with my gun-barrel. No one saw me do it — that's true enough — but I'm saying I did it. Is that enough?"

"Mister Ramsey," the judge paused, moved his two old books a little, and looked uncomfortable. "You don't have to admit a thing. It's up to this court to inquire into the case, just as it's up to the Sheriff to present the facts."

"He won't prove it, Your Honour. He can't. But I'm telling you I hung Lem Cameron. I'll tell you why, too. He and his brothers caught the best friend I've ever had, alone in my barn. They took Pat Reilly and lynched him, just because he was turning out some horses for me. Hung old Pat — one of the finest men in the Paiute Valley — for no other reason than because he was doing me a favour and they wanted my hide for shooting a henchman of theirs — who happened also to be my brother, Jay."

Mort's face was flushed; his eyes glassy. Perspiration stood out like transparent pearls on his upper lip. The new shirt Tassie had bought for him was wilting with moisture. He held up his gun-hand and motioned with it.

"I found Pat hanging to the back of my barn. That was before I knew I hadn't killed my brother. And I found this Lem Cameron lying in ambush for me in the willows near my barn. He was using Pat's body as a lure to draw me in so's he could kill me. Your Honour — the only reason I'm here on trial for lynching Lem Cameron and he isn't here in my place for bushwhacking me is because I didn't fall for his bait. After I captured him he made a fight of it. In self-defence I hit him on the head. After that — I hung him in Pat's place."

When Mort stopped speaking there wasn't a sound in the office. Every eye was on him and stayed that way until the Circuit Rider shook himself erect after a long interim of deadly quiet.

"Mister Ramsey — would you prefer a trial by jury?"

There was something so controlled, so calm and cold in the way he said it that Tassie had to bite her tongue hard to keep from fainting. She was watching Mort breathlessly when he answered:

"No, Your Honour. I'll abide by your decision."

The judge nodded, hitched himself farther forward and leaned over the desk, gazing at the sheriff. "Sheriff Walsh, in your opinion is the case exactly as stated by the defendant?"

"Yes, Sir; as far as I know, it is."

"I see." The judge flicked through the smaller of his two books and leaned back to read. The rest of the room was as still as death. Time dragged. The sheriff made up a very precise example of a hand-made cigarette, sat there looking longingly at it, not daring to light it. Only once did he raise his eyes, and that was to catch the doctor's glance, hold it for a long second, then let his glance wander over Tassie's tight features and on again to Mort's face.

The girl's face was like chalk. She was holding one small fist within the fingers of her other hand. The knuckles showed white from the silent pressure.

Mort looked straight ahead. His forehead was beaded with sweat. Aside from that he was like granite. The strain was visible in the background of his eyes. That was all.

The bailiff finally stopped writing, leaned back, and gazed around the courtroom; sucked his teeth with an irritating sound and stopped it when at least five sets of eyes glared murder at him.

Mort was staring at the judge when His Honour finally closed the little book, placed it meticulously in front of him and glanced at the row of bleak faces in the room. "Gentlemen — the law of this Territory tries a man according to the legal interpretations of the United States. This is the frontier." When he said that, Bennett, attorney for the Big Sink Stage Company, leaned back, sighed softly, and relaxed.

"I repeat, gentlemen — this is the frontier. The law that's out here isn't always the same law that governs fixed communities in the States. Out here, we mix the extenuating circumstances with the facts, quite often, in arriving at our verdicts. The conduct — like the dress and speech — is often different, and justifiably so."

"Get to the point," L. C. Walsh growled under his breath.

The judge turned and stared at him. "Did you say something, Sheriff?"

"Ah — no, Your Honour."

"Yes; well — it is the considered opinion of this court, gentlemen, and backed up by legal statutes in this book of Territorial Law" — he patted the worn little book with his palm — "that the defendant was called upon to attend to the disposal of an undesirable character in self-defence. Further, this court feels that he acted in the same way that any posseman might have acted under identical circumstances, and — legally, mind you — hung a dangerous criminal who himself, if not directly concerned in a murder, at least was an accessory to it — as well as being guilty of contemplating another murder; only his victim fixed the hell out of him, and hung the intending murderer himself.

"All things considered, then, this court finds the defendant — Morton Ramsey — Not Guilty as charged."

Tassie fainted. Mort caught her and pulled her close to him. He didn't see L. C. Walsh try to light a perfect example of a hand-made cigarette — and break the thing in two in fingers that shook. Nor did he see Deputy Blackwell turn to the doctor and wrinkle-up his nose.

"Doc, f'heck's sake — what's an extenuatin' . . . ?"

He wasn't conscious of anything but Tassie until someone touched his shoulder lightly and he turned to look. The sheriff was standing there with one paw extended.

"Shake, pardner — you made it."

Mort shook. "Will you get a glass of water for Tassie, Sheriff?"

"Sure." Walsh was turning away when the doctor plucked his sleeve surreptitiously. Walsh scowled, looked around hastily and beckoned. The two men disappeared into the cell area beyond the sheriff's office.

"Sheriff: what'll I do with that confession Jay signed that he hung Lem Cameron?"

"Tear the damned thing up," Walsh said crisply, "and don't ever open your stingy little trap about it again. That's the ace-in-

239

the-hole we didn't need after all."

The doctor nodded and stood there uncomfortably while the sheriff dipped up a cup of water from the water barrel, then he tugged at Walsh's coat. "Wait a minute. That's for Tassie, isn't it?" Walsh nodded stonily. "Here: I just happened to have a wee dram with me. Pour a little in her water. Make her feel a hundred per cent better."

"Pour it yourself," Walsh said, holding the cup out.

They went back into the office and found it deserted but for the bailiff and the Circuit Rider. His Honour was smoking a potent, eye-stinging black cigar, and scowling through the smoke at the cramped notes the bailiff had taken down. Both men looked up when the sheriff handed Mort the water. Tassie swallowed a little and stifled a cough. Mort smiled at her. She looked into his face for a scared moment, then kissed him fervently. The onlookers were more startled than abashed. Mort pulled free and smiled at the judge.

"Your Honour — I don't reckon it's right for a man to thank the —"

The judge emitted a burst of black smoke and scowled. "You can't thank me for doing my duty, Mister Ramsey. I wouldn't be interested in hearing it."

Mort nodded. "I figured it'd be about like that."

"But," the judge said, "what are you going to do about the young lady? She doesn't look very fit to me."

"Judge, I'm going to marry her."

"That so?" the judge said. "Well, since I'm right here and it won't take very long — and if everyone's agreeable — maybe we ought to tie that knot right now. Mister Ramsey, have you a dollar on you?"

"Young lady — uh — what's her name?"

Mort felt the fire coming into his face. "Miss Tassie Clement."

"Yes; well — Miss Tassie Clement, are you willin'?"

"Oh, yes, Your Honour."

The judge motioned to the sheriff. "Take his dollar and give it to the bailiff, will you, Sheriff?"

Walsh reached out with a cupped hand for the cartwheel, got it, and handed it to the bailiff. The judge watched the transaction with steely eyes, saw the dollar safely into the custody of his clerk, and picked up the larger of his two books.

"Can you stand, Mister Ramsey?"

"For this I can, Judge."

Sheriff Walsh helped on one side and Tassie held him tightly on the other side.

The Circuit Rider laid aside his black cigar, ran a hand quickly through his mop of hair, and squinted in a professional manner.

"I'll make it brief, folks. He's pretty banged-up for standing through a long ceremony."

And he did; running through the marriage ritual with both solemnity and haste. It may have been a ludicrous marriage ceremony in many ways, but to Tassie and Mort Ramsey it never was — not even when it was a dim memory, years and years later.

Lauran Paine, who under his own name and various pseudonyms has written over 900 books, was born in Duluth, Minnesota, a descendant of the Revolutionary War patriot and author, Thomas Paine. His family moved to California when he was at an early age and his apprenticeship as a Western writer came about through the years he spent in the livestock trade, rodeos, and even motion pictures where he served as an extra because of his expert horsemanship in several films starring movie cowboy Johnny Mack Brown. In the late 1930s, Paine trapped wild horses in northern Arizona and even, for a time, worked as a professional farrier. Paine came to know the Old West through the eyes of many who had been born in the previous century and he learned that Western life had been very different from the way it was portrayed on the screen. "I knew men who had killed other men," he later recalled. "But they were the exceptions. Prior to and during the Depression, people were just too busy eking out an existence to indulge in Saturday-night brawls." He served in the U.S. Navy in the Second

World War and began writing for Western pulp magazines following his discharge. It is interesting to note that all of his earliest novels (written under his own name and the pseudonym Mark Carrel) were published in the British market and he soon had as strong a following in that country as in the United States. Paine's Western fiction is characterized by strong plots, authenticity, an apparently effortless ability to construct situation and character, and a preference for building his stories upon a solid foundation of historical fact. *Adobe Empire* (1956), remains one of his best novels. It is a fictionalized account of the last twenty years in the life of trader William Bent and, in an off-trail way, has a melancholy, bittersweet texture that is not easily forgotten. *Moon Prairie* (1950), first published in the United States in 1994, is a memorable story set during the mountain man period of the frontier. In later novels such as *The Homesteaders* (1986) or *The Open Range Men* (1990), he showed that the special magic and power of his stories and characters had only matured along with his basic themes of changing times, changing attitudes, learning from experience, respecting nature, and the yearning for a simpler, more moderate way of life. Recent Western novels include *Tears of The Heart*, *Lockwood*, and *The White Bird*.

We hope you have enjoyed this Large Print book. Other Thorndike Press or Chivers Press Large Print books are available at your library or directly from the publishers.

For more information about current and up-coming titles, please call or write, without obligation, to:

Thorndike Press
P.O. Box 159
Thorndike, Maine 04986 USA
Tel. (800) 257-5157

OR

Chivers Press Limited
Windsor Bridge Road
Bath BA2 3AX
England
Tel. (0225) 335336

All our Large Print titles are designed for easy reading, and all our books are made to last.